A SECOND CHANCE FOR A DANCER

CAROLYN MILLER

Visit Carolyn Miller at www.carolynmillerauthor.com

Copyright © 2026 by Carolyn Miller

All rights reserved.

No part of this book may be reproduced in any form or by any electronic or mechanical means, including information storage and retrieval systems, without written permission from the author, except for the use of brief quotations in a book review.

Cover Art by KT Designs

CHAPTER 1

Winnipeg, Manitoba

Three Creek Ranch could never look like this.

Poppy James smiled as her little ballerinas tiptoed toward her, hands upraised, smiles broad, their pink tutus quivering as they sought to stay on their toes. "Now hold." She held her fingers up: one, two, three, four, five, then closed them in a fist, the cue to drop and move into their next position, just in time with the next bar of the music from *The Nutcracker*.

This, their second last rehearsal before the summer showcase of the Donovan Dance Studio, was all about fine-tuning those little details that would help make their concert sing. Not that there was literal singing; this was an all dancing concert. All the different kinds of dance their studio offered would be on display—ballet, tap, jazz, ballroom and more. And since her friend and founder of the studio Bailey Donovan's stint on *Dance Off Canada* had won her millions of fans—and the heart of her dance partner, Luc Blanchard—the studio had to put on a good show. People expected it. The parents wanted to see their little angels succeed, which meant many late hours sewing costumes and painting sets so their performance could be spectacular. Even some of Luc's hockey-playing teammates had rolled up their sleeves to help. Which was great, even if some of the single dudes had seemed a little too eager to chat with Poppy.

Please. Bailey and Luc might be perfectly happily married, but Poppy didn't need some man clogging up her life. She had enough to do as it was, running classes here in the Winnipeg studio, rehearsing for her own performance. She certainly didn't need a man who would only lie to her and say things that would make her do things she'd regret. Like *he* had—

"Miss Poppy." One of the sweet girls raised her hand. "Why are you angry with us?"

"Angry? Sweetheart, I'm not angry."

"Your face is angry."

Oh. She consciously relaxed her facial muscles. Smiled. "I'm so sorry. Is that better?"

The little blonde nodded.

Regret shafted through her. She was usually much better at keeping focused. She forced herself to pay attention, trapping thoughts that might lead her astray. "Right, well, Miss Poppy is very happy with you all. You all look very beautiful." Her smile grew warmer as she glanced at Maybelle, the little girl with Down's Syndrome who had a modified program. No way did Poppy or Bailey want anyone to feel excluded from participation, just because she might not fit the typical ballet aesthetic.

When she and Bailey had first opened the studio six years ago, they had agreed to keep the prices low to allow all kinds of people to participate. Dance could be expensive, with all the shoes and apparel and costumes to buy on top of the lessons. Keeping costs down allowed for more to attend. Sure, they might not have the elite status of some of the other ballet schools in the city, but as Jesus followers, she and Bailey were conscious that just as Jesus accepted all kinds of people, so they and their studio should too.

And she strived to do so. Except for one particular person who had said one thing then proved to be quite another and—

Stop! She refocused with effort. "Now, let's take it from the top. Are we ready?"

She drew the little girls into line, tapped her phone, and the Tchaikovsky piece began again.

"Oh, they're so darling!" one of the grandmothers gushed after the class had concluded. "It's going to be a wonderful night."

"That's the goal."

"I've invited all our family members."

"Oh!" Oh dear. "That's great. We might need to see if we can get a bigger venue for next year, because I'm fairly sure we're at capacity already." And while spreading the word was awesome, if people wanted to come but couldn't get a seat then they'd have a problem. Clearly Bailey had underestimated the power of her public profile as a fan favorite on *Dance Off* and wife of the Winnipeg NHL team's captain.

"Oh, but can you squeeze in a couple more? Pretty please?"

"I'll look over the ticket sales tonight and let you know."

"Oh, thank you. That would be wonderful."

"Sure thing."

Her cheeks relaxed as the last of the little girls and their carers left, releasing her to a solid few minutes to practice for her own solo. When Bailey had said that due to popular demand she and Luc would reprise a few dance moves from their time on the show, Poppy had realized this was a chance for her to show her own stuff, too.

A second chance for this dancer to prove she should be considered by Winnipeg's leading dance company to dance for them, and thus finally live her dream of dancing across the stages of the world.

Bailey had once done that—dancing in England and Europe. And Poppy had long yearned for the chance to live a bigger life than what she'd always known. She saw her siblings living out their dreams and wished she could do the same: travel the world, taste and see the new experiences offered by living overseas. She could do this. At twenty-five she wasn't too old, even though she'd be up against younger dancers. But still, she believed that God could open the right doors at the right time, so if He wanted her to do this then He could open the right ones. And the fact that Marcel Mouseaux had agreed to come to watch her *had* to mean that God wanted this door opened. Marcel wouldn't have agreed to come otherwise.

So she practiced her grand jetes and arabesques, spinning around in that classic move everyone associated with a music box—one leg outstretched, arms up. She'd be wearing a white tutu and pointe shoes, and provided she could nail the jump, she'd be showing Marcel exactly why she'd fit in his dance company.

She completed the jump—yes!—and concluded the movement, relief filling her.

Applause came from the studio door where Bailey stood with a grin. "You're looking good, Poppy."

"I'm feeling good. I just hope I can nail that on Saturday night."

"You'll be fine."

God bless Bailey. She'd been nothing but a rock of support ever since Poppy had first broached the idea of auditioning for Marcel, saying it was time for Poppy to live out her dreams, and not just feel like she was obliged to support Bailey's own. And while starting the dance studio had been a shared dream, it was far more Bailey's vision than Poppy's. Over the past few years she'd stepped in and out then back in as the studio's finances and needs allowed, and Bailey had said if Poppy didn't get into Marcel's troupe, then she'd always be welcome to teach here. But whether she wanted to continue to do that, she didn't know anymore. Poppy loved her kids, but had always had the desire to do more, *be* more, rather than be the youngest in a family of high achievers and always feel like the least talented one.

Panic rose. What would she do if she didn't get in? Teach for the rest of her life in someone else's studio? Something else? How could she ever feel seen for herself, and not just for being the sister or friend of someone more famous?

"Poppy, God's got you, remember?" Bailey said gently.

She nodded, sucked in a breath and pushed the panic down. A little, anyway. While it might technically be true that God had her, there were things she'd done that meant she could never have the same level of naïve confidence that Bailey owned. Sure, Bailey's own life hadn't been filled with only roses and sunshine, but that had been more about circumstances that happened to her, not situations she'd deliberately gone into with her eyes open.

So while she hoped that God would be kind, she wasn't exactly living with rock-solid assurance. Because she knew the day would come when there would be a reckoning for her sins. She just hoped that wasn't this Saturday.

S\ATURDAY

So far so good.

Poppy silently applauded as the little girls trooped off backstage, their faces lit in grins as wide as their pink tutus. She high-fived them. "You were awesome! Well done. So beautiful!"

"You look beautiful!" Emmeline whispered.

"Aww, thanks sweetie."

She checked that no stray hairs had escaped the crop-duster-worthy amounts of hairspray lacquered on her head. She needed to look perfect, perform flawlessly, and maybe Marcel would agree to take her on. She'd seen that he'd arrived during the intermission—a busy man like him did not have time for watching all kinds of amateurs. But there was nothing like a live performance to really get the juices flowing.

As Bailey introduced the next performance, giving Poppy a nice little spiel designed to reinforce to Marcel that Poppy was the real deal, she moved into position on center stage and closed her eyes.

"God is with you," she reminded herself. What happened in the next five minutes was up to Him. She'd trained her heart and body out; what Marcel saw next would be a yay or nay to her future dreams. And she would have to trust God, regardless.

Bailey finished speaking, applause filled the room as the curtain slowly lifted. She glanced at where her mom sat in the front row, Marcel in the center aisle seat just behind. Then—she blinked. Surely not. What was *he* doing here?

Trepidation filled her, and she almost missed the cue as the opening bars of the Swan Lake recording drifted through the loudspeakers. No. *Focus.* But why was he here? Refocus.

Her arms moved into position and she began the movements, up en pointe. Normally performed as a pas de deux, she and Bailey had modified the piece to suit her, knowing the famous piece of music would be enough for people to resonate with it and enjoy. She'd wondered about whether to do the Dying Swan scene, but while that scene required so much control up on her toes nearly the whole time, this modified piece allowed a greater range of movement.

She moved into the first arabesque, then a pirouette, followed by a leap.

Normally she would blur the faces of the audience, but Marcel was there. And so was—

No! Think about what you have to do!

She regained focus, spinning her way into the trickier part

of her program. Spin, another spin, then *land the jump and you'll be golden.*

She moved into position for the setup, her gaze flicking out to the audience. Marcel was watching intently, so she made every movement of her fingers count. She had to sell the idea of loss, of longing, or regret. Something she knew all too well, thanks to the man who sat behind Marcel, arms crossed, eyes focused on her. Why had he come?

Stop it! She moved into position, gathering speed, then spun into position, propelling herself up en pointe. This was her opportunity, her moment to shine. She caught a glimpse of stage lights, faces, a sneer. She missed her cue. Her stomach tensed. And braced with her arms, before the shock of the awkward landing absorbed the snap of her leg as she fell.

Red Deer, *Alberta*
Monday

"Jake, I know you probably have a fairly good idea about what I've asked you in here for today."

Hope lit Jakob Guillemette's heart as he shot Mr. Cuttrey, the founder and CEO of Cuttrey Engineering Industries, an awkward smile. "I wasn't sure, but I am hoping."

"Jake, congratulations. You've got the job."

"Really?"

Dave Cuttrey nodded. "You were the best candidate, and the one who has proved himself over time. So congratulations on your promotion."

"Wow." Fireworks lit his chest. Promotion? Heading up the new factory site in Canmore wasn't a mere promotion. It was the opportunity of a lifetime. "Sir, I really appreciate your faith in me."

"Well, I like to give people who have served me faithfully opportunities when I can. And over the past ten years you've proved yourself as somebody I can trust. You're honest, you're smart, you take initiative—within reason. All qualities I need for someone to take this role."

All qualities he'd once been accused of as lacking. His heart pinged with age-old regret, and he had to force a smile as Dave continued.

"We had candidates apply from outside the company, but I prefer to go with someone I know and trust, so you were the obvious choice."

"Thank you sir. I can't tell you how much I appreciate you trusting me with this project."

"Now it will be a lot of extra hours, but I know you can manage."

He nodded. "Absolutely." With no wife or girlfriend to consider he had hours of spare time, so he'd put in extra hours until his eyes bled. "Whatever you want sir, I'm happy to oblige."

"I know." He stretched out a hand. "How about we go and make this official over lunch? Does Giorgio's sound good?"

Red Deer's best Italian restaurant? "Sounds great."

LATER, as he drove to his parents—he knew Mom would want to see him when he told her the news—he mulled over the words, and that discomfiting twinge he'd felt. Huh. God must have done a few things in his life if others could now see what *she* sure hadn't three years ago. He wished she could see him now. Seemed like God was in the miracle-working business after all.

He turned into the driveway of his mom and dad's small acreage, noting his brother Ryan's car parked as well. See, God really was in the business of doing unexpected things, considering the woman Ryan had married. Gothic-loving Sylvie, broken as all get-out, had somehow turned out to be a rock star of a wife. Ryan had never been happier. And now she was pregnant, it was like Mom thought the sun poured out of her. Everything was "Sylvie this" or "Ryan that." Well, maybe for once he wouldn't be the second-rate brother, even if he was first born.

He went inside, kissed Sylvie on the cheek, thumped Ryan on the back, then clasped his mom in a hug.

"What's this for?" she squeaked, pulling back with a laugh.

He grinned as her eyes rounded.

"You got it?"

"I got it."

"Oh my goodness! Praise the Lord!"

He laughed as she flung herself at him, nodding to his brother who looked puzzled. Ryan and Sylvie lived in Edmonton, and as Ryan's team were still licking their wounds after their playoff exit, they'd decided to head south and say hi. So the fact that Jake for once had something exciting to share felt like poetic justice for all the times he'd had to grin and bear Ryan's exciting news. Like getting scouted for the NHL. Drafted in the second round. Like watching from the sidelines as his younger brother played with top-tier guys like McHale and he was forced to swallow envy. Like his brother's pay—twenty times his and counting.

Even the fact Ryan had met someone who made him light up in a way Jake had never known—apart from that stupid ill-advised fling three years ago—drew envy. Sylvie was definitely not his type—he'd always preferred petite blondes, especially those with striking blue-green eyes—although Jake had always appreciated a healthy dose of snark. But it seemed like Ryan was winning in life again while he was left thumbs-upping from the sidelines. And he hated this envy, slithering around in his heart and gut, whispering while he tried to sleep. It was easier when Ryan wasn't around. Everything was. Like getting his mom to notice him, instead of fixating on Ryan or Sylvie or their soon-to-be-born baby.

"So what's the news?" Ryan asked.

"Don't you remember?" Mom beamed. "He got the job."

"What job?"

Typical. "You're looking at the new manager of the Cuttrey Industries factory in Canmore."

"Canmore?" Ryan blinked. "You're moving?"

"Well, yeah. You can't exactly run a factory when you live two and half hours away."

"Wow. Well, good for you!"

"Congratulations, Jake," Sylvie added. "I'm really pleased for you."

"Thanks." Satisfaction steamed through him. "Hey, we should celebrate."

His mom beamed. "Absolutely!"

He pushed back his shoulders. He'd finally proved himself. For once, he'd actually outshone his brother and got something right.

LATER THAT NIGHT at Red Deer's top steakhouse—eating too much the way he had today and he'd end up looking like his dad —he'd chit-chatted his way through what the job, the move, would mean, and all the logistics of relocation. It was going well.

Then Ryan glanced at him. "You know, I could put in a word with Franklin James about the best neighborhood to live in, and churches. His family lives not too far from there."

Jake's insides froze. He raised his glass unsteadily, took a long sip to avoid answering straight away. "I'll be fine."

"You sure?" Ryan asked. "I don't mind."

"I said I'm fine."

Judging from the way Mom, Dad and Sylvie stared at him, that hadn't come out sounding fine.

"Whoa, what's with you? I was only trying to help."

"I don't need your help." He gritted out a smile. "Thanks, all the same."

"'Kay." Ryan shrugged, glancing at his phone as it lit up.

Sylvie eyed Jake through narrowing eyes, the same way she did whenever Jake teased Ryan, like she'd appointed herself his avenging angel, and nobody dare mess with her husband otherwise she'd slap them down. It didn't matter how many times he'd laughed it off as brotherly tease. She still thought they should avoid it.

Ryan whistled.

"What is it?" Sylvie asked.

Ryan showed her his phone. "Speaking of Franklin, remember his youngest sister, Poppy?"

Jake's heart tensed. He could never forget.

"I think I met her at their wedding," Sylvie said. "She's the dancer, right?"

Right.

"What about her? Is she okay?" Mom asked.

Ryan shook his head. "Franklin's asked us to pray. She had an accident on Saturday night and broke her leg. It's pretty bad."

His head whipped up. Nobody was paying attention to him. As usual. "What happened?"

Ryan glanced at him. "Looks like she hurt herself while performing."

"Oh, a broken leg would be so bad for a dancer," Mom said. "How is she going to cope?"

And just like that, the focus shifted off him, thanks to Ryan once again.

And while he was sorry for Poppy, he couldn't help but feel a tiny smidge of resentment at the woman who had once again stolen his thunder. Just like she had stolen his heart and his self-respect, all those years ago.

CHAPTER 2

"No. No way. That can't be true." Poppy shifted higher in the hospital bed, her leg shrieking in protest.

The doctor eyed her patiently, her mom looking on with worried wide eyes. "I'm really sorry Poppy, but the x-rays are conclusive. The fall shattered your right tibia thanks to years of stress. The x-ray appears to show the beginnings of dozens of tiny stress fractures, so it was only a matter of time before something catastrophic like this happened."

And of course it had to happen during the showcase, right in front of Marcel. All because she'd gotten distracted by a man who looked like the Voldemort of her life. Anger rose. Her hands fisted. How *dare* he attend her show, knowing he'd distract her?

"And I'm sorry, but you're going to need several months of therapy."

"Months?" Forget her leg shattering; her heart was breaking too. Marcel would *never* take her on now. What was she going to do? This was more than a fractured ankle or broken bone in her foot that required a moonboot. The plaster encasing her right leg meant she wouldn't be able to move without assistance, let alone work. "What on earth am I going to do for the next three months? Watch Netflix on the couch?"

Mom's face held sorrow, just as it had since Poppy remembered waking from the stage after that first moment of blinding pain. As the curtains had hastily lowered, and the screams from the audience echoed her own, Mom had been there, Bailey too, an ambulance summoned while she swam in and out of consciousness. All she knew was that she'd seen the liar, then landed badly. Which meant she could pin all of this on him.

Mom gently squeezed her hand. "Honey, you won't be able to stay in your apartment."

"What?"

"There are too many stairs." Mom explained gently.

"Too many—? Oh."

"You'll need to stay with someone who can help you with your rehab."

That ruled Bailey out. Bailey might love her, but she loved her husband more, and Poppy didn't want to intrude on their newlywed status. She'd encountered a few too many spicy kisses in the past year that would draw a blush if she was a blushing kind of girl. Besides, the encounters she'd had with Bailey's family didn't exactly bring cozy vibes. "What am I going to do?"

"You'll come home with us, to the ranch."

"But Mom, that's so far away."

"I know honey. This won't be easy."

Emotion filled her eyes. None of this was going to be easy. Easy was Saturday afternoon, pre-fall. Now was only pain and trouble.

The doctor took some time to talk through options, both surgery and transport, but it seemed the best option was to pay for a long distance patient transfer service. Fourteen hours on the road would be no picnic, and, "It's going to cost so much."

And her parents might own one of Alberta's largest ranches, but they weren't exactly loaded.

"Franklin said he'd pay. He's praying, and got the guys praying for you."

Tears heated anew. As nice as it was to have people praying for her, they wouldn't have to if Ryan's stupid brother hadn't showed up like he had. Her hands clenched. She hoped he felt bad for the rest of his days. He deserved to, making her fall like this. Although it was weird how he'd shown up then just disappeared again, not making any effort to reach out, even to apologize. Surely if he'd come all that way after all this time then he'd actually have the guts to come and talk to her. The fact he hadn't proved just how much of a coward he was. The fact he hadn't apologized proved he was the total opposite of a gentleman.

Enough! She wiped her eyes, forced herself to take several deep breaths. Okay. This situation wasn't ideal, but dancers knew they sometimes might have to pivot to something new when adversity came their way. Like Bailey had taken shifts in a coffee shop when the studio had struggled to pay its bills. And now adversity had come Poppy's way she had the choice to resent it and live in self pity or use it to fire up within. Which only left one real choice.

The nurse returned with new pain-relieving medication, and Poppy forced a tear-stained smile for her mom as the drugs took effect. But in the wash of sensation between pain and ease, one thing remained clear. She'd never forgive the man who had made her lose focus. Lose focus both this past weekend and three years ago. And, as her eyes closed, she resolved within: she'd do all she could to make him pay.

"Now, Mr. Guillemette, I think you'd like this next offering." The realtor flashed him a smile.

Jake nodded, fidgeting with his tie. So many things to get used to. Like being called Mr. Guillemette for starters. Wearing a suit and tie. Dave Cuttrey had insisted Jake needed to dress to look the part of a factory manager and represent him well. So Jake had needed to buy a couple of new suits and shoes and stuff that really wasn't his style. But while stepping into this new role felt like adopting a part, it also made him feel more confident, like he really was the person who could afford to live in the places Suzy kept showing him. Which he supposed his new salary meant he could afford. But so much house for just one man seemed a little pretentious. Even if it was part of the package that Dave was wanting him to invest in.

"It's all about how you're perceived," Dave had said in their meeting two days ago. "If you're living in a dump of an apartment, people aren't going to believe this is a company worth dealing with. If they know you live in one of the more expensive areas, they're going to believe you're legitimate, that you've bought a place as a long term investment, which means they'll believe we're worth investing in too."

Jake wasn't one hundred percent sure about the legitimacy of Dave's reasoning, but he was sure of one thing. He liked being looked at as smart, as someone whose acquaintanceship was worth cultivating, someone worthy of respect. And it didn't hurt when the realtor showing him around had a nice smile, and nice legs.

Suzy pointed to another house, a little smaller than the previous one. This looked more his speed. He didn't want a house bigger than his folks, but this looked good.

The brown clad house sat on a small lot, but the striking snow-capped granite of the Three Sisters mountains could be seen from the front yard. A small bow window poked out in the front living area, which ran into the timber kitchen stained a nice honey oak. The kitchen led through onto the back porch and yard, which again shared an impressive view of this section of the Rockies. The yard was small and on a slight incline, which allowed for a basement under half the house. Three bedrooms, two baths, the house wasn't too big, but it seemed sturdy. He could see himself living here, gazing out at the mountains in the summer, skiing those very mountains in the winter. It wasn't too far from Banff, so the place could be rented out too if necessary.

"So, what do you think?" Suzy asked.

He nodded, checking the fireplace. A place here would need great heating. "It's got potential."

"Right? And it's not too far from your factory."

Only three miles away. He was no slouch, but he'd really prefer to not have to make a long drive in winter to get to work.

"And it's a lovely neighborhood. Very quiet. Lots of young families."

Yeah, in his experience 'very quiet' didn't always seem to be the vibe with young families. The opposite often seemed true.

"Give it a good look over," Suzy continued. "I know the price may seem a little high but it's worth it for what you get. And the owner is quite anxious to sell. His daughter has recently moved to Vancouver, and he's missing his family a lot."

He nodded again.

"And it's just a short walk to a nearby elementary school, a convenience store, a café and other local shops. And across the street is the Cougar Creek pathway which is perfect for a stroll, cycle or walk into town."

Did she think he was married with a family to need a school and all those things? "It's just me," he mumbled.

"Well, that's still perfect!" Her white smile almost blinded him. "You won't regret purchasing this home. It will set you up for the future."

Yeah, that would require having a girlfriend who might one

day agree to being more. And given the way he'd been scarred three years ago, he wasn't in any hurry to get it wrong again.

"Well, if you give me the paperwork, I'll investigate."

"Wonderful!" She beamed another huge smile at him, and he found a small one in return, which only made hers wider. He wasn't used to this amount of attention and effort from a woman, although it was probably because she was counting her commission. The houses here were pretty pricey, and if it wasn't that this was on the company's dime then he wouldn't have dared look.

"Okay then. Thank you for your time."

He nodded, accepted the paperwork, and paid attention as she informed him which of the nearby cafes had the best coffee in town. "Thanks."

"And can I say how excited we are to know your factory is moving to Canmore. We might be considered by some to be a seasonal town, but there will always be plenty of people thankful for jobs that are year round."

"Dave Cuttrey was aware of that in picking the site."

"Well, I do hope to hear from you again soon." She smiled. "Enjoy your coffee at the Summit."

"Thanks."

As she locked up, he got back in his truck and reversed slowly. He didn't want his entry to town marked by running over any of the locals. He drove to the recommended café, got a coffee as suggested, and took it outside to a table that overlooked the creek. Sure, this place was beautiful in the summer, but already he could tell it was something of a tourist trap too. There were a lot of snow hire places, and stores suggesting that catering for visitors was what this town lived on. So while establishing the new branch of Cuttrey Industries here might seem a little weird to some, it probably would be a blessing to the community. They'd need at least two dozen workers, and all of that would pay off in supporting local businesses.

A SECOND CHANCE FOR A DANCER

"Everything okay out here?" a brunette in her twenties asked.

"Yep." He nodded to the coffee. "It's good."

She beamed. "We think so too. Hope we see you again." She winked.

He found a small smile, but still felt uneasy. Women didn't wink at him. Especially pretty ones. But maybe he could consider this a fresh start in lots of ways.

His phone flashed with a message from the realtor.

> Great to meet you, Jake. Looking forward to hearing from you soon.

He tapped out a reply, gratitude rising within for Dave Cuttrey and his willingness to contribute towards the cost of his senior manager's housing.

The factory coming here would be a blessing. Just as he hoped a new change would prove for him. Finally, a chance to prove himself, to not carry the weight of any expectations apart from meeting those held by Dave. There might be a lot unknown, but this was something he was sure of. This new change was a God-given opportunity for him to live again. And maybe, finally, leave the regrets of the past behind.

IT WAS MUCH LATER that day when he hit the freeway again, watching the familiar road signs and landscapes flash by. A spot-lit sign for Three Creek Ranch rushed by. Huh. That must be new. His stomach knotted. He slowly exhaled. Driving the two and half hours between Red Deer and Canmore was getting a little boring, but at least it had given him a lot of time to think. And not just about all the aspects of his new role and accommodation, but about other things as well. Like how hearing the news about Poppy had gnawed new pain in his heart.

He'd thought he was over her. Thought that sorry chapter in

his life was done. But every night when he closed his eyes he glimpsed that picture Ryan had on his phone of her lying on the stage dressed in her white tutu, looking as broken as her leg obviously was, her beautiful features captured in a moment of pure agony. Her face looked like his heart had felt after she'd stomped on it three years ago.

He'd repented for how he'd thought on first hearing the news of her accident. She didn't deserve it. Ryan's latest report from Franklin had suggested she'd be unable to walk for at least three months, and had retreated to Three Creek Ranch with her folks to recover. Which meant every time he traveled this road he passed the turn-off to where she was.

Not that she'd ever want to see him. She'd said as much three years ago, and her words had burned deep in his soul.

"You're nothing but a liar and a cheat. You've got nothing to offer anyone, no ambition, nothing. I can't believe I was so stupid to fall for you."

His fingers tapped the wheel. Yeah, he hadn't been able to believe it at the time, either. Why would such a young, smart, pretty babe like her fall for a factory-working hick like him? Because in an effort to taste a different life he'd paid way too much for a haircut at one of those hipster barber places, then dressed up in a suit, and attended a play in Calgary. And there, without the constant comparisons to his brother, without any expectations from anyone at all, he'd shucked off his usual manner and acted the part of the suave man about town he'd always kind of wished he could be.

The one who could smile at a pretty woman and see her respond. The one who could talk and not stammer when she came over. The one who might not understand the play too much but pretended enough so that during intermission he'd been able to convince her to meet him afterward for a drink, which had ramped up to two, then three, then a dinner date the next day. And all the time he'd been struck by wonder at what this felt like. Conscious of the other guys who looked at him with jealousy because Jake had the most beautiful woman on his arm for once. Finally knowing what it was like to be envied. So this was what his brother felt like.

The attraction between himself and Poppy had been mutual, had burned hot, until it quickly blazed into something he'd wished it hadn't. Then when he'd found out what she hadn't told him… His gut wrenched. No way would she ever want to see him. It was best to stay away.

CHAPTER 3

The sound of a rooster crowing wove through the mists of dreams. Weird dreams, crazy dreams, featuring everyone from Marcel to Franklin to Ryan Guillemette's brother. Poppy blinked awake, thankful to dispel that last memory, and rubbed her eyes at the unfamiliar sight. That's right. She was back home, here in her not-bedroom at Three Creek Ranch.

"Shut up," she mumbled, as the rooster kept crowing. Unlike her siblings, dawn was never her friend. She was the one who liked to stay up late; Cassie and Jess and Franklin were all early birds, just like their parents. It was enough to make her sometimes wonder if the stork had placed her in the wrong family. It wasn't enough that she didn't look like her sisters, but she wasn't like them either. They were practical and hands-on; she was creative and more craftsy. They were all plainspoken—okay, blunt—but her sisters were naturally nice and interested in people, whereas she knew herself well enough to know she wasn't always. There had been times she might think she'd been hardened by what had happened three years ago, but she'd always had a merciless streak. Kind-hearted folk might call it 'competitive'. She'd justified it as focused and driven. And sure, Jess with her vet studies knew all about being driven, but Jess had learned a lot in the past year when her work as a vet had almost crushed her. Jess was doing much better now, working four days a week while making time for Tom Chavez, Franklin's teammate and friend, who had proved the ultimate friend-to-more in recent times.

"Sweetheart?"

"Hi Mom."

Miranda the cat slunk in, eyeing Poppy with her disdainful eye, as if wondering what she was doing sleeping in the living room like this.

"Don't look at me like that," she groused at Miranda. "There are too many steps to go upstairs."

"Oh, honey. I hope you weren't too uncomfortable."

"It was fine."

The way her mom looked at her suggested that Poppy's tone had told the real truth. Okay, so it would've been nicer after travelling nearly fifteen hours by road to ease her aches and pain by sleeping in her own bed. But that wasn't to be. Instead, she'd arrived home to discover that Cassie and Jess had made up a bed in the living area, and decorated the space with dozens of get well cards, along with two bouquets of get well flowers, both of which were next to the TV.

"At least this way, you'll be in the thick of things and able to watch as much TV as you like," Jess had said.

Hmm. She would have much preferred to have hidden away in her room, like Jess had when she'd had her meltdown last year. But there was a difference between wanting to stay in bed because she wished to avoid people, and wanting to avoid people but resenting the fact she had to stay in bed.

Although Jess was right. Being down here meant she could be in the thick of the action. Well, not quite the thick of it, but at least her wheelchair could be maneuvered to most of the downstairs places. And at least there was a downstairs washroom she could use too.

"Would you like some breakfast?" her mom asked.

"Not yet. It's still too early." She yawned to emphasize the fact.

"Okay."

Her mom left and Poppy glanced around the room, spotting the mood board Cassie had left there. Her heart panged. That's right. Cassie was due to get married in a few weeks, which meant Poppy would be wearing a stupid ugly cast on her leg in all the photos. Tears pricked.

She'd never liked the thought that the others called her vain, but yes, she was a little. And she'd been looking forward to wearing a dress that showed she'd worked hard for the body she had, that the muscles she wore had been earned by years of blood, sweat and tears. Dancers didn't put their bodies and toes through torture without wanting to reap some of the benefits, like looking good in a pretty dress. And now, she couldn't.

A knock came at the door. Well, the entryway, anyway. One of the downsides of being forced to stay in the living room was not having a door to provide any privacy.

Cassie stood there. "Good morning. I came to see how the invalid was doing."

"I'm awake."

"That's a first at this hour."

Hmph. "Why are you looking so happy at this time of the day? The sun is barely up."

"I'm always happy at this time of the day. Have you ever seen a sunrise?"

She scowled which drew Cassie's laugh. "Oh, you're still as adorable as ever when you pull that face."

"I'm not going to look very adorable at your wedding."

"Ah, so that's it."

Poppy sighed, grimacing as she tried to sit upright.

"Here, let me help."

Cassie moved closer and helped draw Poppy upright, placing a pillow behind her back. How she hated being dependent on others.

"I realized this morning I'm going to be wearing this whopping big cast on my leg for all your photos."

"Not *all* my photos. You won't be in some of them."

"Ha ha, yeah, very funny. You know what I mean."

Cassie sank onto the edge of the coffee table. "Come on. We can make sure that the photos are slightly different."

She sighed. "I won't be able to be your bridesmaid."

Cassie winced. "Yeah, that will be a little hard to wheel you down the aisle."

She'd been advised not to put any weight on her leg. So instead of making the most of her chance to impress all the movie stars at the wedding some were calling Hollywood's wedding of the year, she'd be stuck on the sidelines, watching others shine. Again.

And she'd be alone. Still.

Tears filled her eyes and she dashed them away. Tiredness, pain and disappointment were a lethal combination. "I *hate* being this emotional. "

"Welcome to the club."

"No, it's all alright for you to sit there and mock, but you'll be the star of the show and so busy with Harrison you won't even notice that I'll be sitting there like a dummy with no one to talk to."

"Please. You'll be sitting there like a queen, getting waited on hand and foot."

She pressed her lips together to withhold a retort. Nobody liked a complainer, herself least of all. But she'd *really* wanted to meet some of Harrison's Hollywood friends. If the situation with Marcel wasn't going to work out, then a Plan B by way of getting to know some people who might need a dancer could be helpful. But they wouldn't want a dancer who couldn't even stand.

Cassie smiled sympathetically. "Want a cup of tea?"

"Actually, I need a bathroom break."

"Ah, the fun times begin."

"Yep." She emphasized the *p* with a pop.

After that ingloriously embarrassing moment was endured, she settled back in her bed-couch, while Cassie reiterated her earlier offer to make Poppy a cup of tea.

"Yes. Please."

Cassie exited, and Poppy's attention snagged on the mood board, her thoughts drifting to their conversation before.

Memories flashed of Franklin and Hannah's wedding, when she'd danced and shown off just a little. But amid her clever and strong siblings it had felt nice to finally have some place where they could acknowledge her superiority in one small area at least. And if that made her vain and shallow, then so be it. A girl had to find those moments to feel good about herself. And it hadn't hurt to have drawn some eyes, especially of some of Franklin's teammates, who until then had always seemed to regard her as a little girl.

But she was twenty-five now, and wanted to be known in her own right. So now, without dancing, what would she be known for? Being snarky? Being mean? Her bottom lip wobbled. Maybe she really was the little girl she insisted she wasn't, with all this crying she kept on doing.

"You're being stupid," she muttered to herself.

"Who is being stupid?" Mom asked, holding Poppy's tea.

She shook her head, a frog in her throat preventing her from answering.

"I think she's a little disappointed about the wedding." Cassie's brow puckered. "If it really means that much to you, we could see about postponing it."

"What?"

"Oh, Cassie, no," Mom protested. "It's only weeks away, and arrangements have been made."

"I know, but if Poppy is going to be upset…"

Her chest heated. She knew that Cassie meant well, but she didn't want to sound like a little sulking child. It would be hard enough to find a new identity, at least for the next three months, without adding crybaby youngest sister to the mix.

"I *won't* be upset. I'm just having a moment, okay?"

"Poppy—"

"I know you and Harrison have waited long enough, so do it. I'll get over it. But I'm allowed to be disappointed, aren't I?"

"Of course you are." Mom looked at her, her sympathy plain.

She ducked her head, warming her hands on the mug of hot tea.

"We're praying for you, honey."

She nodded, her lips pressed together. Prayers were nice, but sometimes it seemed like they were only words, much like people who sent 'good thoughts.' Like, what good did sending thoughts actually do? Where did good thoughts go? She, who had prayed and tried to follow God for years knew only too well that sometimes the best intentions didn't work out. And while she'd had her secret backsliding moments, she'd still always known God was there. Which was probably what had made that particular situation so tricky. God had been there when she'd been doing things she shouldn't have.

Mom placed a hand on Poppy's shoulder. "And we'll see what we can do about making some tweaks to things so you can participate."

"Don't go changing things for me."

The raised-brows looks her mom and sister gave her suggested that those words had come out a little more petulant than she intended.

"I didn't mean it to sound like that. I just mean that I don't want you to alter the things that you want to happen because of me."

"Poppy, you're my sister and I love you. I want you to be involved as much as you can be, okay?"

"Okay." She tucked in her bottom lip. "I'm sorry."

"Hey, I know this is hard. But we'll find a way."

She accepted her sister's hug—Poppy wasn't much of a hugger—and hoped their prayers worked. Because clearly God did not think hers were worth listening to.

"Yes, that's right," Jake said, the road to Red Deer now so familiar he could practically drive it with his eyes shut. "They think it will be ready next week."

Dave Cuttrey whistled. "That's amazing."

"I think it's like road construction. They're motivated to get it done in the summer, especially because it's going to provide jobs for the community, so the community is on board to getting it done."

"Okay, well, good job. Sounds like things are well on track."

"I hope so."

They discussed a few more things and then Dave had to answer another call. "Keep up the good work."

"That's the plan."

Dave ended the call and Jake smiled. So far, so good. Of course, it was one thing to oversee the construction of a factory building. It would be another to actually run it successfully. But considering he planned to implement every single one of Dave's instructions based on the operations in Red Deer, it shouldn't be too problematic. He hoped.

The fuel gauge flashed, signaling he'd need to make a stop

soon. All this driving was adding to the wear and tear of his car. But at least it was a fairly straightforward journey, highway nearly all the way.

He pulled off at the nearest service center, pulling in behind a white Lexus. As he refueled he glanced across at the guy filling up in front. His stomach tensed. Those broad shoulders made him look a bit like someone he'd met a few times now. Someone he'd felt awkward meeting, ever since he'd first learned the man was his brother's friend, and Poppy was his sister.

The man glanced back, and—his stomach fell—yep, it was Franklin James.

Franklin's brow puckered, as if in recognition, like he was wondering why Jake hadn't responded, so Jake nodded.

Franklin grinned. "Hey, you're Ryan's brother, right?"

"Jake."

Franklin clicked his fingers. "I remember. We met at their wedding."

And on a few other occasions, but okay.

"What are the chances, eh?"

Very slim.

"What are you doing out here? I thought you were up from Red Deer way."

"I'm moving to Canmore for work."

"Really? Now that's a sweet part of the world. Everyone always talks about how awesome Banff is, but I've always thought Canmore just as pretty."

"It is that."

Jake finished filling up, and they both went inside and paid.

"So, who do you know there?"

"In Canmore? Not a soul yet. We're hiring a team so I'll be getting to know some folk soon. I've been waiting for the factory to be completed with its fit out."

"You heading back to Red Deer now?"

"Yep."

"Well, if you're back this way, you should call in sometime."

He nodded, knowing those words held more kindness than real truth, knowing his nod held the same.

Franklin sighed. "I don't know if Ryan told you, but my youngest sister got hurt pretty bad a week ago."

His throat dried. He coughed, trying to find a speck of moisture. "Yeah, I heard. H-how is she?"

"Not doing too great."

His heart stretched tight. "I heard she busted her leg."

"Yeah, pretty thoroughly. We kind of expect people to sometimes break legs in hockey, not ballet. Crazy, huh?"

"Super crazy," he muttered.

"Well, I'll tell her you wished her well."

"Oh. Uh, maybe don't—"

Oh man. How could he finish that sentence without sounding like a fool? *Don't tell her you bumped into me because she hates my guts. Don't tell her, because if you do and she spills the beans on why she hates my guts, then you and all the rest of your family are likely to hate my guts too.* Yeah, there was no good way to end that sentence.

Franklin eyed him, head tilted.

"Um, I meant, I hope she gets better soon. I'm praying for her." Those things were true.

"Thanks, man. Appreciate it. We'll take every prayer we can get."

Yeah, he was pretty sure Franklin wouldn't take Jake's prayers if he knew what Jake had done.

Franklin held out a fist like he wanted a fist bump.

Huh. He thought that was something only little kids did, hence the need to tease Ryan when he did the same. He obliged him anyway.

"Good to see you. Drive safe. And I mean it. If you're doing that trip and need a break sometime, call by the ranch. Three Creek Ranch. You know it?"

"I know of it." Ryan and Sylvie had mentioned loving their visit there for Franklin's wedding. And Poppy had mentioned it several times too.

"Well, hopefully we can get you out there one day."

He nodded. Franklin might hope that, but Jake could bet his left arm that Poppy would hope he'd never darken even the driveway of her home. That made a visit there a solid no.

Franklin opened the door of his vehicle. "Drive safe now, okay?"

"You too."

Franklin grinned and soon drove away.

Leaving Jake nervous and tense, worried about just what Poppy's big brother might say to her. And just what Franklin might do if he ever learned the truth about what the two of them had done.

He keyed his ignition. "Lord, I don't know how many times I need to say I'm sorry, but I am. I really am. Please forgive me, and help Poppy forgive me. And please, please heal her leg soon, and heal her heart. In Jesus's name, Amen."

CHAPTER 4

Why did itches always have to be in the most hard-to-reach spot? If only she could press her nails through the cast and scratch. But no. The itch refused to be scratched, just like another itch in her heart that had refused to go away either. At least there was a chance this itch might get sorted one day.

Itches, pain, broken sleep. Would the list of aches and ailments ever go away?

She eased her leg from where it rested stretched out in front of her, but still the throbbing refused to go away. There was nothing for it. She popped some more meds, sipped some water. She'd learned she needed to be careful in how much liquid she took in, as getting rid of it was a seriously unfun part of this broken leg business. But then, there were so many unpleasant parts of this business.

Like the phone call she'd had with Bailey yesterday, where she'd had to explain she would be unlikely to return until September at the earliest.

"September?"

It was one thing to skip out on Bailey just as she was

about to commence her summer filming for *Dance Off Canada*. Bailey had understood, saying that they simply wouldn't offer their usual summer programs. But it was quite another for Poppy to be absent at the busiest time of year, when school returned, and *Dance Off's* screening on TV would ensure a higher-than-usual volume of students all desperate to learn dance from one of Canada's favorite dancers.

"I'm so sorry."

"No, honey. We'll figure something out. I'll see about hiring another teacher or two. It's okay."

It wasn't okay. So many people were having to make new arrangements because of Poppy's injury. First Cassie with her wedding, and now Bailey with the dance classes. And it was all because of *Jake*. Heat rose. How dare he come to her recital and make her lose her concentration? She eyed her broken leg. This was all his fault.

Benji, the golden Labrador that Jess shared with Tom, wandered in, pausing as he noticed her white lump of leg. "Hi boy." She scratched his head, and he leaned his jaw on her lap. At least someone around her was sympathetic. Not that the humans weren't, but she got the feeling that just as this was wearing on her, it was starting to wear their patience thin too. Or maybe those pressed lips was more due to her bad attitude.

"I wish I could run outside with you," she mumbled, stroking Benji's soft head.

"Hey." Jess entered. "Here he is. Hello, boy," she said, as Benji woofed.

"And here I am too."

"I can see that." Jess shot her a small smile. "How are you feeling?"

"It's so hot. And I never knew how itchy a cast could make me feel. It's like there's a constant itch there."

"That's probably in your head." Jess might have studied

veterinary science, but she was the most clued-in concerning medical conditions around here.

"It still feels itchy," Poppy complained.

"Then you probably need to distract yourself. I know: seeing Cassie is at the western town, why don't we talk bachelorette party ideas?"

"Sure."

"Come on." Jess rolled her eyes. "That hardly sounds like you're excited."

"Well, I can hardly offer anything exciting when I am stuck here, can I?"

"Are you feeling sorry for yourself again?"

"Look, I'm just being a realist. I can't move, in case you've forgotten."

"I know," Jess said, patience lining her voice and face. "But it doesn't mean we can't still come up with something exciting to do for Cassie. We just need to be a little bit more creative about it, and we all know that creativity is your specialty."

"That's true," she mumbled.

"So that's your job. Come up with the perfect plan for Cassie."

"But it can't be too like what we did for Hannah." Poppy gestured to her leg. "Not that I'll be doing any swimming in the river."

"We could still do a high tea and a movie."

"As long as it's not a dumb movie."

Jess's eyes lit. "Actually, that could be perfect. We could watch all of Harrison's movies. Wasn't he shirtless in some beach one?"

Poppy laughed. Her laughter sounded creaky, probably from disuse. "That'd be awesome. She'd be so embarrassed."

"See? So that's *exactly* the kind of thing we need to do."

Poppy's smile faded. "It's just really hard not being able to do the things I'd planned to do."

"Tell me about it. Actually, don't. I've been there, done that, got the T-shirt."

Yes, she had. Well, not a literal T-shirt, but last year's breakdown had seen Jess struggle to find her mental and emotional equilibrium for some time.

"It's really hard when you feel like you're letting people down," Jess said. "But most people will understand. You have to learn to be kind to yourself, but also recognize there are times when you need to make an effort. I'm pretty sure someone we both know and love said that to me last year." She winked.

Poppy grimaced. "It's one thing to say it. Another thing to live it."

"Ain't that the truth?"

Poppy loved both her sisters, but sometimes Jess seemed to understand her in a way Cassie never would. Maybe it was because they were the two youngest, and conscious of the bond shared between Franklin and Cassie. Of course, Poppy knew Franklin had a special spot for her too, even though sometimes her sisters said it was because she was the spoiled brat of the family. Whatever. She'd use her status as youngest of the James siblings to her advantage.

Her phone buzzed. She glanced at the screen. "I wonder what Franklin wants?"

"You won't have to wonder if you answer your phone."

Poppy wrinkled her nose at her sister and answered the call. "Franklin. It's me and Jess is here too. You're on speakerphone."

"Hi Poppy, hey Jess. How are you feeling, Poppy?"

"Fan*tas*tic."

He chuckled. "Yeah, I can tell."

"How are you and Hannah?"

"Yep, all good."

Hannah had experienced a miscarriage several months ago. And while she couldn't imagine Hannah ever wanting to give up her career as a TV sports journalist, her distress last Christmas had suggested maybe they did want a baby. But as they hadn't heard anything more on that front, she wasn't going to pry. They could share that news if they wanted to.

"Hey, just wanted to let you know that I saw Bree and Mike Vaughan yesterday, and they wanted you to know that they're praying for you," Franklin continued.

"Thanks." Her heart warmed. So she wasn't forgotten completely by the outside world. Sure, many of her students and their parents had sent little messages, cards and gifts but that had trickled off. To have people still inquire after her meant a lot.

"Oh, and this is really random. You'll never guess who I bumped into the other day."

"Well if you think it's random, I'm hardly likely to guess, am I?"

He chuckled again. "Remember Ryan Guillemette? Plays for Edmonton."

"Yes, Franklin." She rolled her eyes at her sister who rolled her own eyes back. Of course, now Jess was dating Tom Chavez she'd been sucked into the hockey world a little more.

"Anyway," Franklin continued, "I saw his brother the other day."

Her heart froze. Jess's eyebrows rose.

"Jake Guillemette."

The name was like a hammer on her heart. She unhooked her gaze from Jess.

"Anyway, he sent his good wishes. Told me he's praying for you."

She closed her eyes. Nope. No way. He didn't get to cause her accident and then say he was *praying* for her. Her fingers fisted. How dare he?

"Poppy? Are you still there?"

"Poppy?" Jess asked. "What's wrong?"

Everything. "Nothing." She opened her eyes, grimaced.

Jess frowned. "No, that definitely looks like something is wrong."

"Jess? Is Poppy okay?" Franklin asked.

"I don't think so," Jess replied. "Poppy?"

"Sorry." She faked a smile. "I'm a little tired, that's all."

Jess's gaze narrowed, searching her like she was hunting for the truth. "I'm not convinced that's it, but okay. If you insist."

"I insist."

"Anyway, I thought you'd like to know that people are thinking of you," Franklin said.

Oh, but she didn't want *that* particular person thinking of her.

"It's just random, having someone you've never met say he's praying for you."

"I think it's sweet," Jess said.

"I thought it was really nice," Franklin agreed. "But then they are a good value family."

"Mm-hm."

"Poppy? Are you still there?"

She was so glad this was not a video call. It was just a shame her sister was there, reading her every facial move. "Thanks for letting me know, Franklin. Hey, I gotta go. Bathroom break." That'd be sure to get him off the phone.

Sure enough, a second later he murmured, "Don't let me keep you."

"Say hi to Hannah for me."

"And me," Jess sang out.

"Will do. Catch up soon."

"Thanks for calling," Poppy said, then ended the call.

"Excuse me?" Jess said. "What was that about?"

"What was what about? I do need to go to the bathroom."

Jess's brow lowered, but she helped her up anyway.

A little later, Poppy was hoping she'd done enough to deflect

Jess's interest, but it seemed her sister was as determined as Benji was when presented with a bone.

"You seemed upset before," Jess said, without preamble.

"Upset?"

Jess sighed. "Don't play games with me, Poppy. Last year I was the master of game playing, so I can tell when something is wrong. And you were fine until Franklin said something about Ryan's brother."

Her fingers involuntarily twitched again.

Jess's eyes widened. "Do you know him?"

Obviously she hadn't. Not really. He'd presented himself one way, then she'd realized what she thought she knew was all a lie. "No."

"Why do I get the feeling that you're lying to me?"

"Because you're not very trusting?"

"Maybe right now it's because you're not acting very trustworthy. You *do* know him, don't you?"

"I don't want to talk about this."

"Oh, we are now *definitely* talking about this. Who is he? How did you meet? What happened?"

No. No way was she going to spill any tea on this.

"Jake..." Jess's eyes widened. "Is this Jake the Snake?"

Anger rippled through her. Okay, so she may have accidentally spilled a clue or two last year. It didn't mean she needed to share anything more. Except... "Jake the Snake or Jake the Fake, take your pick. It's much the same."

"Oh, I'm picking both option A *and* B, thank you. Is this something we need Cassie here for as well?"

"Nope."

Jess's forehead creased. "Mom? Franklin? Hannah?"

"I have nothing to say about any of this."

"That's not true, and we both know it. Come on. Tell your big sister, and then you can tell me what you want me to do about it."

"There's nothing to say," Poppy insisted.

"Yes, there clearly is. Like, how do you know Ryan's brother? Wait, isn't he older than Ryan?"

She pressed her lips together, gaze sliding from Jess as she nodded.

"Oh my gosh! Did you date him?"

How she wished she could say no. Instead, she dipped her chin a quarter inch.

"Oh, Poppy. He must be what—at least ten years older than you?"

"Eight."

"He's a cradle snatcher!"

Exactly what he'd accused himself of. Once he had found out how old she was.

She'd never really known what the expression 'aghast' looked like. Until that moment.

He'd gone pale, fingers raking his hair, his stubbly cheeks, while she'd lain there, ashamed not just about what she'd done, but at letting him believe a lie. That look of horror had stayed with her, and was her last memory of him. Until the Saturday night two weeks ago.

"How did you meet?" Jess asked, folding her arms like a tree that would never move. Heaven knew Poppy sure couldn't. Which left her two choices: she could ignore her sister or finally succumb.

Poppy sighed, then told her in a low voice about going to a play in Calgary, meeting a handsome man who called himself Jakob, who then bought her drinks while she'd pretended to like them. She hadn't, but she did like the effect of being with this charming man who seemed to think she was charming too. At least, he'd said so. And laughed at her jokes. And she'd laughed at his. Then wondered how in all the world she could feel like she'd finally met someone who seemed to hold a similar sense of snarky humor yet still had faith. And that had been great, until the next day when they had dinner, and shared a kiss—

"Oh, Poppy." Jess's eyes were huge.

"Well, not everyone wants to wait as long as Tom did with you," she snarked.

"Apparently," Jess muttered.

"Fine. If you don't want to know—"

"I do! I want to know if I need to hurt this man, because it seems like he's hurt you."

"He did."

"How?"

She swallowed, and told her the more convenient truth. "Because after we broke up, he suddenly showed up in Winnipeg at the concert." She blinked back tears. "I got distracted because I saw him there. Jess, he was sitting right behind Marcel, you know, the guy whose troupe I'm supposed to be dancing with right now, instead of being stuck here."

"Oh my gosh. He was there? He must've wanted to talk to you."

"Except he didn't. And I sure as heck don't want to talk to him."

Jess nodded slowly. "But… that doesn't explain why you called him a fake or a snake before."

No way was she going to admit just how stupid she had been. "He wasn't who he said he was."

"He's not Ryan's brother?"

"He is, but he wasn't this smart sophisticated man."

"No? Why, what does he do?"

"He works in a factory."

Jess blinked. "Are you serious?"

"Yes!" Finally, someone could see her point.

Jess's lips twitched, then she burst into laughter.

"What?"

"Oh my gosh. You're still as much of a snob as ever."

"What? No, I'm not."

"Oh, you are. Wow." Jess's phone buzzed and she looked at it. "I can't believe you almost had me believing he really did hurt you."

"But he did! He showed up at the concert—"

"Sorry, Poppy, I gotta take this. But it looks like you're going to have to work on your forgiveness."

"What?" How dare she?

But Jess was already walking away, talking on the phone.

Leaving her seething with resentment, with hurt and dismay. Forgive Jake? There was no way she was going to do that. Not today. She eyed her leg. Not ever.

CHAPTER 5

*J*ake rubbed his eyes and powered down the window to get some cool air. Another too-long drive had him yawning, and he needed to stay awake, even though he had another ninety minutes before he'd reach Red Deer. He glanced across the highway to where a spot-lit sign announced Three Creek Ranch.

His stomach tensed, his thoughts flicking back to Franklin and his invitation for Jake to visit someday. Yeah. If pigs flew, maybe.

He cranked up the music, but the heavy rock didn't drown out his thoughts. Thoughts of her. Regrets. Shame. Guilt. He might pray for her, but his prayers seemed to fall flat. Restlessness ate at him, as it had ever since he'd seen Franklin, like a long stagnant inner pool had finally been stirred.

He took the road that led past Calgary, and the high rises all lit up at night. He'd given up his apartment thanks to the logistics of traveling back and forth, and returning to Red Deer now meant staying with his folks. This drive was growing old, and he couldn't wait until he was finally settled in Canmore. But until then he'd have to keep his boss happy and do the things required of him.

Weight pressed in, his mind sinking deeper under the responsibilities he had to carry. And carry he would, as he needed to prove he was worthy of the gig.

The next song came on, one he'd always hated, so he changed stations, but it was much the same. Noise, more noise, nothing that settled his soul.

Turn it off, a little voice said.

So he did. Drove five kilometers before, once again, his mind flicked back to her, to her horror when she realized he wasn't the executive he'd kind of made himself out to be, but a humble factory floor worker.

"You work at a *factory*?"

"Yeah." His chin had jutted. "That's nothing to be ashamed of."

"But… that's not how you came across."

He'd scowled. "Careful. You're starting to sound prejudiced, like you think there's something wrong with that."

And while she hadn't said the words, her face had spoken volumes. Like, the fact she was disgusted at giving herself to someone who clearly wasn't who she'd wanted him to be.

Talk about a kick to the heart. Her reaction might've spurred him on to finally seek advancement at work, resulting in a promotion to factory floor manager, then impressing Dave Cuttrey enough to be given more responsibility. But it had also been enough to put him off ever hoping for a relationship, second guessing himself about everything. What he wore, what he did, how he appeared. He'd retreated into working hard to prove her wrong, and spending too much time online gaming and in worlds that only fed his insecurities. And while he knew he was a Christian, he'd played around on the surface there too, doing the routines, trying to look the same, like the good Christian boy his mom had raised, even while he knew he was limping underneath, his soul bruised and battered.

And now, ever since Franklin had issued that invitation, it felt like a wound had been prodded, and he realized there was pus and pain festering underneath, and had been there for many years.

By the time he pulled into Red Deer he was exhausted. Physically, mentally, emotionally. This was weight he couldn't carry anymore.

He pulled into his mom and dad's and parked, weariness so heavy on him he could barely move. Still, a man couldn't sleep out here. Well, probably he could but he'd be in all kinds of pain tomorrow, so he found enough energy to stir and go inside. A light was on in the kitchen, so after dropping his keys on the entryway table, he went there.

Food smells greeted him, a million times better than anything he could pick up via drive-thru. "Hey Mom."

She turned, taking him in with a wrinkled brow. "Jakey, oh, you look exhausted."

"Yeah."

She came to give him a hug, and he lingered a little longer than normal, knowing he needed some human arms tonight. There was only so much a man could do on his own before he felt isolated and alone. And seeing he'd felt isolated and alone for many years, despite a loving family, he was hungry to know that he wasn't as alone as he might feel.

Mom pulled back, studied him. "Are you wanting dinner?"

"I'm almost too tired to eat."

"You need to eat, get something into you. You're getting thin." She patted his cheek. "You'll be no good if you get sick from being too tired all the time."

Mom should know, having trained a million years ago as a nurse. So he obeyed as she sat him at the table and reheated lasagna and fussed over him.

His thoughts tumbled to what it must be like to have his own family, to have his own wife fuss over him. Then sank deeper, knowing that what he'd done made that impossible for him. He couldn't be trusted. He'd proved that before. Women wouldn't want him. No woman he wanted, that was.

He ate mechanically, did his best to answer his mom's questions without answering what she really wanted to hear. He barely had strength to keep his head up, let alone spill the truths that she probably deserved to hear. But he couldn't. Not tonight anyway.

"Jakey, are you sure this job is right for you? You're so tired I can barely get a word of sense out of you."

"It's not for too much longer," he promised.

"I hope not. Are you sure you're not better off staying in Canmore?"

"Dave wants to meet with me face-to-face. And it's hard with his times clashing with mine to actually find the time and space."

She nodded. "And as he is your boss I can understand you don't want to rock the boat."

"Exactly."

"Still, you need to be careful. I don't want you putting your health at risk for the sake of a job."

"Like Ryan does?"

Her nose wrinkled. "Touche. I do worry about that boy. But he does have good medical professionals on that team. You don't."

"Apart from you," he said affectionately.

"Hmm. Well, you don't need to be a hockey star to get injured at work. Look at what happened to that ballet dancer friend of Ryan's."

Protest reared within. He ducked his head. Poppy had been Jake's friend, not Ryan's. Even if she wasn't now, and likely didn't want to have anything to do with either Guillemette brother now.

"Jakob?"

Oh, she was pulling out the big guns now, using his proper name like that. He was in trouble. She only ever pulled out his full name when he was in trouble. Or about to be.

She eyed him, her expression holding some of that fierceness she'd been known for.

He shook his head, emotion too close to the surface.

"What's wrong?"

"I..." He shrugged, as the hopelessness of his experience pressed deeper. As if he could tell his mother what he'd done. She'd be shocked, devastated, the disappointment would know no end. She might've embraced Sylvie into the family fold, but there was a difference between accepting a woman with a broken past who hadn't known Jesus to realizing her own son had been wearing a mask these past years and might as well be the Prodigal son.

"Jake, I love you."

"I love you too, Ma." He couldn't do this anymore. He buried his face in his hands and sank his head onto the kitchen table.

Tiredness swam through his brain. Weariness at the secret he'd kept locked up far too long that it was now poisoning his soul. Regret and shame spun around, like ice dancers, carving blades into ice. It felt like he would never lose this shame. He'd tried to pray it out, tried to prove to God that he wasn't that man anymore. It hadn't worked.

Moisture seeped from under his closed eyelids. Great, now he was crying like a girl. He sucked in a steadying breath, then released. Did it again. Then again.

"Jake, whatever is wrong, I want you to know that I love you, and God loves you. Nothing is too hard for Him."

Emotion pricked again, swelling in his chest, his throat.

She rubbed his back, and like a genie with a lamp, out it

finally came. But he kept his eyes closed, so he wouldn't have to see her disappointment.

"It's not work, it's her."

"Who?"

"Franklin's sister, Poppy. The one who got hurt." His voice was raspy.

"What about her?"

"I hurt her, Ma."

"What do you mean?"

He could barely find the words, but eventually found enough that made sense. He told her about feeling jealous of Ryan, wanting a chance to finally make an impression and turn a girl's head. Meeting Poppy. Kissing Poppy. More than that he wasn't brave enough to admit, but from the look she gave him when he dared peek, she might've guessed.

"She didn't want me. Said I lacked ambition, wasn't smart." Well, she might not have actually said that, but she'd implied it. "And I was too old for her."

"How old was she?"

"Twenty-two."

"When was this?"

"Three years ago."

Mom winced. "You were eight years older."

"Still am."

She didn't smile, only looked at him seriously. "I'm guessing from the way this is eating you up that more than just kissing occurred. No, I don't want to know the details. But if you did something that you promised your future wife you'd save for her then I'm not surprised if this has been hurting you."

For some reason, he felt compelled to say, "I only ever did that with her."

She closed her eyes, her mouth pressed in a tight line. He could basically see the disappointment ricocheting through her.

He and Ryan had always thought she had eyes in the back of her head, but she hadn't seen this one coming.

"I can't pretend I'm not disappointed. But I'm guessing that's nothing to how you feel right now. And probably how she feels too. You said she's a Christian?"

"Yeah," he said tiredly.

"Well, nobody is perfect. And Christians who pretend otherwise are hypocrites."

"I just felt like I took advantage of her, which was never my intention. I thought she was older, and..."

"Yeah, I'm gonna guess there wasn't much thinking going on when other things were going on."

"Mom."

"Oh, don't 'Mom' me. I wasn't born yesterday." She sighed.

That sigh held a weight of disappointment.

"I wonder if this is why I heard this this morning?"

She moved and got her phone, and tapped the screen, then shoved it at him. A preacher was on a video, one he knew his mom liked to listen to. "Mom, I'm too tired."

"You need to listen to this."

She pressed play on the YouTube clip, and the preacher started talking.

"How many times in the Bible do we see God described as a shepherd? In Psalm Twenty-Three we read that the Lord is my shepherd. Jesus, when He tells the parables about the lost coin, the lost son and the lost sheep. Have you ever thought about that? How the shepherd left the ninety-nine sheep and went after the one that was lost. If you think about it, really think about it, it doesn't make sense. No shepherd would leave ninety-nine for the sake of one. They'd cut their losses, and stay and guard the ones that remained. Not seek the one that might never be found. Except this is a picture of what God does for us. What God does for me. What God has done for you."

Jake shivered.

"God loves you so much, loves *you* so much, that He was prepared to leave the ninety-nine for you. He was prepared to sacrifice His own son for you. Because He loves you. You. Me. Everyone in this world. And it's not a matter of being good enough, perfect enough, or even us in our own efforts trying to find God. God is searching for you. God has always been looking for you. He wants you to let yourself be found by Him. He wants to give you rest, He wants to protect you, feed you, look after you. It's not about your own efforts, it's all about His."

Jake propped his head in his hand as he watched the preacher.

"Imagine that lamb that was lost. It's dirty, it's hungry, it's smelly, it knows it's lost. Then imagine how it feels seeing the shepherd that it knows loves him. Shepherds used to sleep out in the fields with the sheep, which is why we have the Christmas stories of shepherds in fields at night watching their flock. The shepherd wants to protect his flock from the predator. He wants to protect you. You don't have to be perfect. You don't have to have it all together. You don't have to look like you have it all together. You just have to let yourself be found by Him, to sink on His shoulders, and rest. Let Him carry you. Let Him give you what you need. Salvation is simply consenting to being found by Him. So let the good Shepherd carry you."

The preacher prayed, but Jake barely heard his words, as the message sank deep within. Tears slipped and he palmed them away. Oh, he knew he was lost, he was dirty, snarled and sin-stained. He was hungry to find hope. And a new job was only a kind of temporary rebrand for his life, a distraction. All it could ever really do was try to mask the pain. It wouldn't actually deal with it. He needed his heart cleansed, once and for all.

Lord, I'm so sorry. I can't do this. I need Your help. Please help me to know Your love.

He took a shaky breath, but not all of the air in the world could prevent a sob from ripping from his lungs. He cried. And he cried some more. And even more, in embarrassing sobbing heaves, until it felt no more tears were left.

But inside… Inside he felt different. A little lighter, a little more hope-filled.

His mom rubbed his back, and handed him the tissue box.

"Thanks." He blew his nose. "Sorry."

"Don't *ever* be sorry for getting yourself right with God."

That was more like the fierce Mama Bear he knew and loved.

He moved to the sink, dunked his head under the water and washed his face. Thank goodness his dad and Ryan weren't around to see—or hear—any of that. He knew a lot of that was due to tiredness, but it had also felt like a necessary release.

"So, what now?" Mom asked.

"It's late, Ma. I can hardly think let alone plan anything."

"I'm gonna guess if you feel this way, then she feels a similar sense of regret too." Her brow creased. "Did you ever get the chance to talk to her?"

He shook his head. They'd never had a chance to talk it out. When they had woken, she had looked so guilty, and accused him of taking advantage. When she told him her age, he realized he had.

"I didn't really talk much back then. But I still feel like I need to see her, ask for her forgiveness." When she might actually hear it, rather than simply react in the heat of guilt and emotion. "Not that I think she'll want to ever see me again." That's what she'd said, anyway.

His mom nodded. "As far as it depends on you, live at peace with others."

"Yeah."

"Let's pray for her," she suggested.

They did, and again he felt like some of the inner heart shards had been buffed a little smoother.

"Buy her the biggest bunch of flowers you can. And chocolates. If she's held onto this pain this long too, then she probably needs some sweetening up."

"I'm so sorry Mom."

"Yeah, I know." She opened her arms.

And just like the Good Shepherd, who left all His other sheep to get one, Jake felt the same sense of love and acceptance in her hug.

"I'm so sorry this has been eating you up," she murmured.

"I feel a bit better now."

"Forgiveness cleanses us, cleans us up. It keeps our hearts soft, because it reminds us we're not perfect. It's when we try to live up to our own inflated ideals of our own goodness that pride gets in and starts to lie to us and hardens our hearts to the truth. The truth is that we all need Jesus. It's just some of us are more willing and ready to be found, while some of those sheep just keep digging deeper in those brambles like they think they'll get themselves out. They won't. They can't. But you have." She stroked his cheek. "I'm proud of you, Son."

Fresh moisture wet his eyes, and he had to blink hard to get it away. "I love you, Mom."

"I love you, too. So does your father. And Ryan. And Sylvie, too. But you know who loves you most of all?"

He nodded. "God."

"*Especially* God. So go to sleep tonight, give this all to Him, and we'll ask Him for some answers and wisdom going forward."

"Thanks, Mom."

God knew Jake needed all the wisdom he could get.

CHAPTER 6

Once upon a time she had been known as Party Poppy, someone who loved a late night and a good time better than most. Despite the best efforts of her sisters to include her in various bachelorette and wedding preparations, these days she felt more like Party Pooper Poppy, and those days of enjoying a party seemed long gone.

Once upon a time, she had also been known as Bossy Poppy. Those days remained. But still, a woman who was forced to lie around had to be pretty blunt about saying what she wanted. Although, now she thought about it, bluntness was a trait she had long owned.

Maybe, being the youngest, she had been privileged in a way her older siblings hadn't. Not spoiled, exactly. Just extra blessed.

She rolled her eyes at herself. Look at how extra blessed she felt now.

Her leg stretched out, the white cast feeling like her own personal tomb of lost dreams. Marcel's recent email had only confirmed what she already knew. That she'd lost her chance to join his dance company as they had found somebody new. So now without that lifeline, what remained? Working with Bailey wasn't exactly a hardship, but it still felt like trying to force some puzzle pieces into a pattern that didn't quite fit. And maybe—if she was completely honest, they hadn't fit for a while now.

Growing up on a ranch, the concept of seasons was one she was familiar enough with. Perhaps working with Bailey was only meant to be for a season, and maybe this season was coming to an end. She glanced at her leg. Maybe it had already come to an end, and she was just starting to realize that.

But if not working with Bailey, then what was she supposed to do with her life? Her leg throbbed, reminding her. What if this was actually a life *altering* injury? She wouldn't know for months, not until the cast was off and she could undergo physical therapy. What if she could never dance again?

A whimper escaped. "God?"

No answer, but that wasn't unexpected. If only God bothered to answer straight away as she would like. But then, patience wasn't a virtue she was familiar with.

Her mom and dad had always been patient, a trait none of their daughters seemed to inherit, although Franklin possessed more than his fair share. Maybe God had used it all up on him and none remained for the rest of them. Certainly none remained by the time Poppy had come along.

Impatience sawed through her on a daily basis. Impatience about how long it took to have someone reply to her messages, or that it took for anyone to realize that when she said she needed to go to the toilet she wasn't joking. Some days, it seemed like she should investigate adult diapers, but that was a humiliation she couldn't articulate, let alone figure out how to facilitate. She couldn't even answer the door, let alone carry a box to the bathroom or hide it upstairs. Ugh. She *hated* being helpless.

Her phone dinged with a notification. Hannah.

> Thinking of you.

Praying hands emoji.

She sent back a heart. See? She could be nice.

But as another long day rolled before her she wondered what she'd do. There was only so much television she could watch, and books, well, it depended on how much she wanted to read. Boredom chewed at her, incessant, like the book bugs she'd found that had chewed through her mum's old copy of *Persuasion*. Nothing held her attention.

Nothing except for this persistent sense of injustice, resentment, a low level kind of seething. Why should she lie here injured, when the man whose fault this was, was still running around the world, happy and free? It wasn't fair. And this was now *twice* he'd hurt her. Back three years ago, and now three weeks ago.

Her lip curled. Maybe she was being unfair, but she didn't think so. Her thoughts spiraled back to the morning after that night she'd always regret. She'd woken, shocked to find an arm across the white of her stomach. Then glanced across and seen dark eyes smiling at her.

"Wh-what happened?"

"Good morning to you too."

No. This wasn't a good morning. None of this was good. She'd shoved off his arm and wrapped the sheet around her, then gingerly peered under it. Bit back a word. Then glanced down at the floor where her clothes—and underwear—lay tossed.

Memories hit. Kissing. Drinking. Fumbling. Darkness. Car. Hotel room. More kissing. More... *more*. Then waking up to this, her head aching, her heart heavy and sore with regrets, as she realized what she'd done in giving away something she'd promised God to keep for her future husband. Shame, horror, and a hangover made for a volatile mix, especially for someone overly prone to wielding truth with a blunt axe.

She'd been mean. Nasty. Blaming him when she'd been just as much at fault.

But still, her heart protested, he should've known better. He was older—scarily older, when she was twenty-two—although now it didn't seem so bad an age difference.

Other memories pinched, like when she and Bailey had discussed the similar age difference between Bailey and Luc. That had been one of Bailey's dad's concerns too, until he saw how good Luc was for Bailey. But it was one thing to counsel another, and quite another to preach it to herself, and believe it.

No, just as she'd believed all these years Jake was a snake, a fake, a rake as bad as the awful ingratiating young Mr. Eliot in *Persuasion*, pretending to be interested in Anne while lying about his true self. Jake Guillemette had done the same, pretending to be one kind of person when he'd been very different. She'd never trust him again.

The back door slammed and she sat up. The footsteps sounded like Mom had returned from picking berries.

"Poppy?"

"In here." Because where else would she be?

"Oh, look. Try these. Don't they taste divine?" Her mom held out a bowl of strawberries.

Poppy picked one, tasted it, the burst of flavor saying this berry was definitely home grown. "It's really good."

Her mom smiled. "There are some good things about being home, aren't there?"

Poppy nodded, fresh shame filling her at her grumbles and complaints. Maybe Grumpy Poppy was another name she'd earned recently. "Thanks for putting up with me."

"You know we love you."

"I love you too," she said gruffly. It felt like a long time since she'd said that.

Her mom smiled. "Do you need a bathroom break? A cup of tea? Coffee?"

"I'd love a bathroom visit." It was always a good idea to take one when they were on offer, regardless of whether it was needed or not. "And maybe a coffee." Although coffee seemed to result in a bathroom break in less than an hour. "Actually, maybe I'll just have water."

"Well, I'll put the kettle on and we'll do the bathroom while it boils."

Ten minutes later she was back in her favorite position, a fresh T-shirt on, the bathroom break resulting in a quick wash via a sponge bath as well. Showers were just too much of a hassle, and when she wasn't doing much anyway, and the air conditioning meant she wasn't getting sweaty, it didn't really matter too much if she didn't shower very often.

"So, what are you going to do today?"

"Mmm, let's see. Nope, nothing new."

"Would you like a jigsaw puzzle?"

She withheld a roll of her eyes. "Mom—"

"No, come on. It might be better than you think."

"I doubt it," she muttered, as her mom collected a bunch of boxes from a shelf.

"Now, which would you prefer? A lighthouse? An English country garden? An Australian sea-scape or the Rockies?"

She huffed out a breath. "I don't care."

"Then have this one." Her mom handed her the English garden one.

She eyed the box with dismay. An English manor house of many windows sat behind a large topiary garden filled with plants, flowers and lengthy hedges. "This looks hard."

"It's a good chance to develop your patience."

"I don't have much of that."

Her mom eyed her. "Exactly."

Her mom helped move things so Poppy could reach easily

and have space to work. She tipped out the plastic pouch that had never been opened. Obviously, others had thought this puzzle too hard, too. Still, as she separated pieces into edges and colors, it felt good to be doing something again. Even if it was as pointless as this.

She'd gotten most of two edges done when a knock came at the door, followed by the doorbell. She muted the music blaring from the TV and yelled, "Mom, someone is at the door."

"Oh! I didn't hear it."

No kidding.

Her mom wiped floury hands on her apron and answered it. Poppy strained to see but couldn't. They didn't get too many visitors out here, and most who came were invited, and knew they didn't need to use the doorbell but could come straight in. So who was this?

She gritted her teeth. What had she come to that she was doing jigsaws like an old lady and the highlight of her day was peering to discover who was at the door?

Low voices met her straining ears, then her mom's "Oh, she's right here."

Panic rose. That could only mean one person: herself. She propped herself up, pinched her cheeks. She hadn't worn makeup in weeks, and barely brushed her hair. What was the point when the only people she saw were family?

"Poppy?" Her mom beamed at her. "There's a young man here with the most enormous bunch of flowers for you."

Her pulse increased. "Who is it?"

Her mom murmured again, and again the low voice trickled to her ears. Who was it? Her mom knew most of the guys who might call in unannounced like this. And none of the others she'd ever dated knew where she lived. Oh, look at her, treating this moment like it was a highlight of her year.

Her mom returned, this time holding the bunch of flowers, which truly were beautiful. The collection of roses, carnations, sunflowers and lilies was so pretty, the bright vibrant colors exactly the kind she liked. None of those pastels for her, which always seemed like sympathy funeral flowers.

"They're so pretty." She took a sniff as her mom held them closer, then whispered, "But who are they from?"

"He says he met Franklin recently, and Franklin said to call in."

"What's his name, Mom?"

"Oh!" Her mom smiled. "His name is Jake Guillemette."

Her heart shriveled. No. No way. "Take them away."

"But Poppy—"

"No. I don't want them. And I don't *ever* want to see him here."

"But he just wants to talk to you. He's come all this way."

"I don't care. See this?" She pointed to her leg. "He's the reason I broke my leg."

Her mom eyed her, then peered back at the door. Thank God the man didn't have enough gall to walk right in. He'd obviously used it all up driving out here in the first place. "Poppy, I really think—"

"No." She folded her arms. "Don't let him in here, Mom. I'm begging you."

Her mother sighed, and again Poppy felt that soul pinch that she was being mean. Then she hardened her heart. No. The man who had broken her heart, her vow to God, her leg—had broken her!—would *never* break her again. She lifted her chin. Never.

JAKE SHUFFLED AT THE DOOR, refusing to cross the threshold, even though Mrs. James had invited him in. He wouldn't dare step across until he knew he was welcome. And judging from the delay, that welcome didn't seem like it was coming today.

He shifted to face the drive, saw the fenced-in cows and red barn, the blue peaks of the Rockies rising in the background. No wonder they had a rocking chair positioned to take in the view. There was peace here, even if he could feel his own tension rise the longer Mrs. James took to return.

But the heart-to-heart he'd had with his mom last week had pushed fresh resolve into him. He'd prayed, then taken time to craft a card of apology, and had taken more time to figure out how best to go about this. Which was why he was here, on his way back to Canmore, when he'd be late for what he'd planned to do, but he'd figured this was more important. He wanted the chance to finally see things healed instead of ignoring things as they festered. But the delay sounded like any thoughts of forgiveness might be too soon for her.

A creak at the step turned him around. The fact Mrs. James still held the flowers, her fallen features gave the answer he'd dreaded.

"I'm so sorry, Jake." She moved to hand them to him.

He stepped back, refusing to accept them. "I bought them for her. If she doesn't want them, I hope you might like them."

"She did say they were very pretty."

He nodded. Before she knew they were from him, he bet. "I know it's presumptuous of me, but I have a card as well. I figured she might not want to see me, so I wrote it. Would… would you mind giving this to her? Maybe one day, if you think she'd just throw it away today."

She studied him for a long moment, her blue-green gaze holding a piercing quality just like he remembered her daughter's as being. "I don't know what's happened, but I do know that my daughter was upset to hear your name."

He nodded. Stubbed the porch with his booted toe. "We dated. Very briefly. It didn't end well. And I've been carrying this in my heart ever since. So I wanted to make things right, as far as I can, anyway." He half-shrugged. "I've been praying for her."

"You're a Christian?"

His lips twisted. "I'm a better one today than I was back then. God's been on my case a while now."

"You said you know Franklin."

"I don't. Not really. Ryan, my brother, he knows him better than me."

"Is... is that how you met my daughter?"

"No. We met in Calgary by chance. And, yeah, I'm sure she will tell you what happened. And most of that will be true. But I am sorry, so sorry. I never meant to—" Stupid emotion rushed up his throat, forcing him to cough, to look away. "Anyway, I'll leave this here. I'm sorry to bother you."

"Wait. Jake? Is that short for Jakob?"

"Yeah." The liar and deceiver. His parents had sure chosen his name well, hadn't they?

"I'm Leonie. I don't think we've met before, have we?"

"No, ma'am." Hadn't he already told her that?

"And yet your face seems familiar."

"Some people think Ryan and I look similar. You might mistake me for him."

"No. I feel like I saw someone like you recently." Her brow cleared. "Were you in Winnipeg lately?"

"No. I haven't left the province in months."

"Oh. Well, I must be mistaken then. Sorry."

He waved it off. "No apology needed." Except his, obviously. "Again, I'm really sorry to bother you. And you can tell Poppy I won't bother her again."

Mrs. James bit her lip, her expression worried, but she nodded.

He left the card on the porch's rocking chair and hurried

away, trying not to look like he wanted to run. He did want to run. He wanted to run and never stop.

For he'd done what he'd thought God wanted him to do, what his mom had encouraged, and now it was up to Poppy to accept or reject as she chose. Well, she'd made her decision pretty clear, hadn't she?

His heart ached, as he got into the vehicle and started the engine.

He wiped at more stupid moisture that had leaked, and glanced back to see Mrs. James still remained on the porch. Which meant she'd probably seen that too. Well, apparently this man didn't have to lower himself any more to reach the depths of humiliation. The only thing that could make this worse would be for her to tell Franklin, who would then tell Ryan, who would laugh at Jake about it for the rest of his days.

But he sensed she wouldn't do that. Her daughter might be stubborn and blunt-spoken, but Mrs. James seemed to wear kindness just like she wore that old-fashioned ruffled apron. Like it was part of her, her identity.

And maybe he was getting soft but he suspected that was something God wanted from him too. A kind heart, a soft heart, willing to be led by Him, even if it made him look like a fool.

But better looking like a fool than being the foolish sheep all broken and tangled up and lost like he had been before. Like he wondered if Poppy remained still.

So he prayed for Poppy, for God to heal her leg and make her whole, and to do the same with her heart and soul, and that any injury he'd caused her would be healed one day. "In Jesus's name."

And as he prayed, his heart softened toward her, which only drew more prayers. Then praise, that God who could forgive the sinner, had chosen to find him and heal the bruises his own actions had placed on his soul.

Something he prayed that Poppy would know soon too.

CHAPTER 7

The flowers stared at her accusingly, just like the envelope that bore her name that had sat there next to the TV cabinet the past two days. When her mom had finally come in, bearing both, a long time after Poppy had rejoiced at hearing Jake's vehicle drive away, anger had pulsed through her. How dare he force her mom to do his dirty work?

She'd protested, but her mom had shaken her head. "This bouquet must have cost hundreds of dollars. I'm not about to throw that away."

"But you don't know what he did."

She realized as her mom looked at her that a statement like that demanded an answer. But she couldn't speak of it. Not yet.

"I don't know what he did," her mom said softly, "but I can assure you he was grieved by it."

"Yeah, right."

"It looked like he might've been crying when he drove away."

What? Her heart pinged. No. Mom must've been mistaken. Guys like him didn't cry. They used and abused and laughed about it later. She glanced away.

"His face looks familiar," her mom mused. "But he said we'd never met."

"He was at the recital, Mom. He was sitting just behind you. He's the reason I broke my leg. I saw him and got distracted and —"

"No, that wasn't him." Her face cleared. "*That's* who it was. I thought he looked familiar, but it was someone who looked like him. Now I think of it, that man was a little rounder-featured and graying at the temples."

"No. That man at the recital was *him*." She stabbed a finger at where Jake's vehicle had driven away.

"No, it wasn't," her mom patiently insisted. "I remember because I dropped my water bottle and he passed it back to me. I remember thinking he was quite a handsome young man, but it's obvious now he was older than your visitor just now."

Poppy had studied her mother. Had she got it wrong? No. She couldn't have. Her mom *had* to have been mistaken.

The jigsaw puzzle was now nearly half completed, but the questions in her mind refused to find answers. Why had Jake come? Was it guilt? She guessed the envelope might hold a clue but she didn't want to risk it. What if it was simply a get well card and he hadn't bothered to beg forgiveness for what had happened in the past? Then again, what if he'd written to beg forgiveness for what had happened in the past and she was forced to actually do something about it?

She didn't want to forgive him. Anger felt safer than letting herself weaken. And she'd been angry for so long that it was hard to imagine herself as anything but this hard brittle shell of a woman who wore a painted smile and projected sassy strength but felt close to dead within. As she had ever since that morning she'd woken up in bed with a man who proved to be a stranger. That man, who had waltzed up to her front door like the past didn't matter.

Except...

Her gaze strayed back to the flowers, still looking perfect even several days later. Mom was right. Those flowers had to have cost a bomb. Way more than what a factory worker could likely afford. Guilt snagged her heart. How judgmental she'd been. That wasn't her, not really. Except the fact it had leaked from her lips suggested perhaps it was.

She bit her lip. She'd said so many horrible things, perhaps because she simply was a horrible person. And even the fact she kept judging him now, blaming him still when Mom said he'd been remorseful. That he'd cried...

Her heart panged, as a little voice asked: *Why else would he go to all this trouble if it wasn't to make amends?* Had she been too harsh? Mom seemed to think so. Mom had plenty of questions, but bless her, hadn't pushed. It was enough that Jess now knew some of it. She didn't want her mother to be disappointed as well.

When Jess had called in yesterday she'd been gobsmacked at the flowers. "Wow. Poppy has a secret admirer, huh?"

Mom had glanced at her, but Poppy refused to answer. Real mature, she knew.

"One of Poppy's former friends dropped them off. A man called Jake."

"Oh!"

The way Jess said it raised Mom's eyebrows, and Poppy thought she caught a little crease of hurt in her eyes. And yes, it felt bad to keep things from her mother, but she didn't want to hurt her like she knew this news would.

She'd mentioned Jake the Snake to her sisters last year, but never anything to her mom. And Jess was the smartest member of the family, and could put two and two together to get enough of the truth, even if Poppy hadn't actually said the words aloud.

And while it was one thing for her sister to guess, it was quite another to admit her failings to her mother. How could she confess her sins? Mom would be crushed.

Still, the envelope taunted. What had he written?

But no. If she opened it, she'd be forced to confront whatever it was he'd written. And she didn't have time for that. Well, she had plenty of time, but not enough will or inclination. Not with everything else that was going on. Like her dad's recent bout of heartburn, which had been serious enough they'd wondered if he needed to go to the doctor. Like Cassie's wedding, which was drawing nearer, and so much remained to be done. Like various family gatherings, and the bachelorette party this weekend, which still needed details finalized.

So much to do, so little time. And there was definitely no time for revisiting the past.

"THIS IS GREAT, POPPY!" Bree Vaughan smiled as Jess and Mom returned with more tiered cake platters holding sweet delights.

"I'm glad you're enjoying yourself. It was a little trickier to manage seeing as I'm stuck in this." She pointed to her cast-wrapped leg.

"And in this warm weather too." Bree's face wore sympathy. "But still, Cassie's having fun, and that's the main thing, right?"

Poppy nodded, glancing over at her sister as she laughed with Hannah and Ainsley Beckett. Ainsley Beckett, the star of the historical drama that filmed on the ranch *As the Heart Draws*—or who had been until recently, when she'd shifted into other roles. She had a TV movie with Jason Streetley that had just released, and another contemporary TV show, a mystery, even though there were plenty of historical fans who had made their position clear that they didn't want to watch her in that kind of role.

As the on-site manager of the western town and movie lot where *As the Heart Draws* had filmed over many years, Cassie had become close with Ainsley who had starred in the show since day one. Which had made her recent withdrawal from the show a little more problematic. Cassie had mentioned that Ainsley had not wanted to upset her, knowing that leaving her role as the sweet schoolmarm might lead to the show being cancelled. Cassie had understood however, and as the show hadn't been cancelled, although viewing numbers were lower this past season, it wasn't a problem. It was good to see some friendships could survive challenges. Even if others seemed to have stretched spider-web thin.

Poppy hadn't heard from Bailey for a while. And while she understood newlyweds might be busy it still hurt a little. Especially when Poppy had gone out of her way and dropped everything to help her friend when Bailey had been called up to be a pro dancer on *Dance Off Canada*. Maybe she was more a situational friend, someone people only liked for a season, then they moved on with their real friends.

"I love the flowers."

Poppy's head jerked up to where Ainsley was fingering the petals. She still couldn't believe they looked so good almost a week on. Cassie, Jess and Mom had said they'd be perfect for helping decorate and make the room look pretty, and she couldn't very well disagree. Even if they still taunted her. Like a gigantic floral guilt trip of what she'd done.

Ainsley glanced at Cassie. "Did Harrison give them to you?"

"They're Poppy's."

"Poppy." Ainsley smiled at her, and again Poppy felt that flicker of resentment that she was stuck here in a chair instead of being nearly as glamorous as the movie star who was talking with her. "I didn't know you had a boyfriend."

"You didn't know because I don't." She cringed as the sourness of her reply was reflected in the surprise on Ainsley's face.

"They're very pretty," Ainsley said softly.

She nodded, pressing her lips together. She didn't want to admit that anything Jake had done was good.

"They're from a secret admirer, right?" Hannah said, joining the conversation, handing Poppy a floral-decorated plate filled with macaroons, scones and sandwiches.

That's what she'd been told, anyway. She'd sworn Mom and Jess to secrecy, and a secret it would remain. The sooner she could forget him the better.

Franklin didn't know either, which was just as well, and she hoped her sisters hadn't spilled the truth to their boyfriends. She didn't need Franklin finding out what had happened. Neither did she want Tom and Harrison knowing either, these men whom she regarded now as mini-Franklins, like brothers who would fight for her if she needed them to. Well, Tom would. She'd seen him throw a few punches in games. Harrison might know some movie punches but could probably still beat Jake-the-snake in a fight if push came to shove.

"So who are these from again?" Brenda, a stuntwoman on *As The Heart Draws*, asked.

Poppy shoved a macaroon in her mouth, and let Hannah answer for her. The less she could lie the better.

She glanced around at where the other woman laughed and poured tea. It wasn't the celebration that Party Poppy might have once thrown, but it was okay.

Somewhere Cassie and Ainsley had managed to find some cardboard cut-outs of Harrison, and these propped around the living room certainly added some fun factor. Various ladies had taken photos with 'him' and used the photo booth in the corner, filled with props and old-time dresses borrowed from the western town set. The others had had fun, even if Poppy could only wear a bonnet and shawl. She could barely manage her crutches, so changing clothes used energy she really couldn't spare. It was enough to figure out how to maneuver the wheelchair.

They spent the rest of the afternoon and evening watching Harrison's movies, eating too much food, drinking too much tea, and even though she had to lie down the whole time, it had gone better than she'd expected. And Cassie was happy, which was the main thing.

Now it was only two weeks until the wedding, when she'd hopefully have figured out how to use crutches so she could hobble down the aisle at least.

And swallow her pride that she'd forever be remembered as the dancer who couldn't dance.

JAKE GLANCED AROUND THE HOUSE. Thank goodness he was finally situated here, having just signed the contract for the rent-to-own agreement for the house he'd now call home. Thanks to Suzy—and Dave, whose bonus pay had allowed him enough to make a deposit to purchase and not stay trapped renting forever—he'd gotten the home he'd walked through, and had moved in what meager possessions he called his own. Even so, the house felt too big for him, and seemed to echo of Jake's failure to have a wife, have a family, but that didn't matter too much, as he was barely home except to sleep. Now that construction on the factory was finished it was time for the real fun stuff to begin.

The workforce would consist of twenty employees, along with several people from the Red Deer site, people who would train and equip those working here. He was kept busy from dawn to past dusk checking and re-checking. He'd never been a systems guy, but in recent weeks he'd really knuckled down to writing lists, copying over the programs and procedures from the Red Deer site, and getting things in order. He had multiple conversations daily with Dave, who had come over earlier this week to check on things.

"It all seems to be tracking as planned," Dave had said, to Jake's relief.

So much responsibility over many aspects meant that there was a lot of potential to have things go wrong. As the manager, he had to sign off on what seemed like dozens of compliance reports, and prove that they were ready to commence production next week. So with the team, he'd done training in occupational health and safety and first aid. Each night he'd go to sleep his mind buzzed with things to add to his to-do lists, before sleep claimed him and he'd dream of her.

He wished she'd agreed to see him last week. Wondered why she hadn't responded to what he'd written on the card. Had she even read it yet? Man, this waiting was hard.

But his mom was praying for him. She was the only one who knew. Well, Dad might now as well, but Ryan didn't. No way did he want his little brother looking down on him, even if he was taller.

Day by day he focused, checked the items off his list. And day by day he prayed, and did his best to give his anxieties to God. Asked God to bless her, to soften her heart, to help him be patient. To remove the thorn in his heart. To let her go, be released from his heart.

And day by day a little bit more of the pain within him healed.

WITH THE CANADA Day holiday rapidly approaching Jake was heading back to Red Deer for the first time in what felt like months. It had only been two weeks, but still, it felt too long. He called his mom as he got in the car. "See you soon, Mom."

"Can't wait Jakey. It'll be so good to have you here again."

"Yeah." It had been too long since he'd been home.

"Drive safe."

"Always. Love you."

The highway yawned before him, and he might've driven it a hundred times before but right now it felt like weight. He was tired, but it felt like more than that. Anxiety rippled along him. Restlessness teased within.

Whether it was his new work role or related to a mistake from long ago, he didn't know. But he wanted to go home to see if missing home was what had caused this inner agitation. Here in Canmore, where he'd had to carve out his new grooves in doing life, meant so much uncertainty. Back in Red Deer he knew exactly how life would roll out.

He stifled a yawn as weariness stole across him again. He had given the new factory's employees a half day in preparation for the national holiday tomorrow which had been gratefully received. But the long hours were catching up with him.

Yawns punctuated the first thirty minutes of travel. He pumped the music higher, but as he neared the turn-off to the ranch, again that sense of disquiet from before stole over him, and he turned the radio off.

His thoughts returned to the last unpleasant encounter. Leonie had been kind enough, clearly not liking the words she'd been forced to tell. Poor lady. It wasn't her fault her daughter held resentment closer than a pet puppy.

"Lord, bless them," he muttered. "Help me be a blessing to them."

The miles passed. He drew closer to the little cross road that would enable him to get to the ranch. Felt the strangest impulse to turn the wheel and go there. He turned away. That was dumb.

Then a sickening squeeze in his stomach was followed by a throbbing in his chest, accompanied by a fresh urge to turn around. His heart pounded, the agitation from earlier doubling, trebling. What was going on? He'd been fine a few minutes ago, then this hit out of nowhere.

"God, I don't know if that's You, but I really don't want to go back there."

So? a little voice seemed to say.

"She made it pretty plain she doesn't want me there."

But what if I want you there? that little voice from before whispered.

He gritted his teeth. "I don't think this is fair."

But still the compulsion to turn around and visit remained. Sweat slicked his fingers. He wasn't scared of her, but didn't want to jeopardize any chance of reconciliation especially when he'd promised that he wouldn't return. Breaking his word like this would only make her mistrust him more.

"God?"

Go.

"Fine."

He slowed, and at the next cross road, did a U-turn and drove back to the ranch. Dread lined his stomach. She hated him. Didn't want to see him. And he was trying to respect her boundaries. He just hoped she understood that God might not respect hers.

This inner urge to go had to be from God, right? It was certainly not anything he wanted to do.

He turned off onto the dirt driveway that led to the ranch. The two-story farmhouse beckoned at the end of the lane. Maybe she wouldn't be home. Maybe she had an appointment. "Lord, if she is there, then please let her be more gracious. I don't know what I'm doing here, so if You don't want me doing this, please give my car a puncture now."

His tires remained steadfast, so he guessed that was God's way of saying keep going.

So he drove, parked and knocked on the front door, as he had ten days' previous. He wiped damp hands down the back of his shorts.

"Come in! It's open."

His heart stuttered. He recognized that voice.

So he swallowed, and obeyed.

He stepped inside a hall paneled with photographs, then paused.

"I'm in here."

Oh, so she didn't know it was him. He braced and went inside.

Then met shocked blue-green eyes. "You!"

CHAPTER 8

*P*oppy's heart shrank as someone moved into view. Far from the florist she'd promised her mom she'd meet with, this was instead the someone she'd vowed never to speak with again. Looked like that vow would prove to be yet another promise she'd break. And of *course* he'd have to see her when she looked like a mess, while he looked like he'd had a glow up. A little leaner than the last time she'd seen him, a few extra years suited him.

She hiked her chin, her eyes narrowing. "You're not the florist."

"Uh, no."

"What are you doing here?"

His gaze slid to hers, the dark eyes as piercing as she remembered. "Hi Poppy."

She didn't dare speak in case she said some words her mom would definitely not like to hear. She was due to come back any moment. She let her eyebrows do the talking instead.

"I, uh, saw Franklin recently, and he mentioned you were injured."

She scoffed. "As if you'd need Franklin to mention that. You were there!"

His head tilted. "Sorry? I was where?"

"At the recital! Why did you come anyway?"

He gestured to the last of the flowers, stubborn sunflowers that refused to wilt or fade. "I came to give you those—"

"No! Why did you go to the recital? Did you want to talk to me?"

"Well, yeah. That's why I came today."

"Oh my gosh." Was the man stupid or something? "At the recital in Winnipeg. Why did you go to Winnipeg?"

His brow creased. "I didn't."

"You did! I saw you there."

"Yeah, no, you didn't. I haven't left the province in months."

Huh. Misgiving struck. His voice, his expression held sincerity. Was her mom right and Poppy had gotten it wrong and mistaken him for someone else? Still, that didn't change the fact that she most definitely had *not* mistaken the identity of the man she'd woken up beside. "What do you want?"

He pressed his lips together, glanced at the envelope she still hadn't opened, now propped on the bookshelf just out of her line of sight so it wouldn't taunt her day and night.

Another niggle stole within. Okay, so she should have read it. But she'd been busy. And... yeah.

She tilted her chin. Inched herself higher in her prone position then folded her arms. Waited. Eyed him like she might Miranda when she brought in a dead mouse.

He shifted awkwardly. "Obviously you don't want to talk, so I'll leave. I thought maybe I was supposed to come here but that seems wrong now."

What was with him? Why would he think he 'had' to come here? Jake was acting really strange. But then, that was only to be expected because the man was strange. Delusional, even.

"Anyway, everything I wanted to say I put in there." He gestured to the envelope.

She shook her head. "I don't want to hear anything you have to say."

His chin dipped. "I figured that. That's why I wrote it down. In case you change your mind one day."

"Please leave."

He turned to go, then paused, glanced back. "I'm really sorry," he finally said. "I guess you haven't read my card, but that's what it said. I'm sorry for hurting you three years ago, and that you got hurt in Winnipeg. I'm sorry for upsetting you the other day, and now. And I hope… I hope one day you'll be able to forgive me."

At the look in his eyes, remorse wormed its way inside. This wasn't the laughing confident man she'd known years ago. This was the man she could see as maybe having teared up when he'd left the other day, just like her mom had said. She clamped her lips together. No way did she want to weaken, make him think she'd let go and let him be free of blame.

She forced her gaze away, staring out the window to the distant Rockies beyond. After a moment he moved, and she heard the front door open then close. And as it closed, something inside buckled as a secret part inside began to wail.

Part of her wanted to call him back. Part of her feared what might happen if she did. If she forgave him, then who could she hold responsible for the biggest mistake of her life? Who could she blame then but herself?

A crash came at the back door.

"Mom?"

She frowned. Why hadn't her mother answered?

"Mom?"

Still no answer. What had happened? Oh, she wished she could stand. Well, she could stand—just—but getting up and down using crutches was so painful. "Mom? Dad? Is that you?"

She grasped her crutches, carefully moved them into position and hauled herself upright. After carefully maneuvering past the coffee table, she began a slow hop down the hall and out through to the kitchen. And saw her father lying on the floor. Then began to scream.

WHY HAD God sent him here when he clearly wasn't wanted? Jake sat in his car, puzzling it out. Had he just misheard what he thought God had said? Heard what he wanted to hear, instead? Oh, who was he kidding? As if God would talk to him. He scrubbed his hands down his face. This was painful. She hated him still. Hadn't opened his card. At least he'd had the chance to say he was sorry and ask for her forgiveness. The ball was in her court now. He'd forgiven her, but the choice was now hers to forgive him, even if it seemed pretty unlikely.

"I don't get it, God," he muttered.

No answer.

Maybe he'd simply been delusional after all. He started his car, reversed from his spot, and steered away. What a mistake this had been.

He was partway down the drive when movement in the rear vision mirror caused him to slow. A figure moved behind him on the porch, waving an arm. Was that Poppy? On crutches?

Then she fell over.

Oh no! Protectiveness rushed up. He slowed then spun the car around. Was she okay? Had she relented after all? Maybe this was his chance…

He exited the vehicle, and rushed toward her, where she was struggling to get upright. "Poppy?" He reached out a hand to help her up.

She pushed him away, pointing back inside the house. "It's my dad! He's inside, in the kitchen. I think he's had a heart attack. I can't do CPR."

"Where's your phone?"

"My phone?"

"You need to call 911."

"Oh! It's in there."

He rushed inside to the room he figured she'd been in before, snatched up her phone and hurried back to hand it to her. Then raced down the hall to the kitchen. There, an older man he figured must be Poppy's dad lay, one hand clutched to his shoulder, ominously still.

Jake dropped to his knees. "Sir?"

Man. He'd just trained for this. What did he have to do first? Call 911. Well, he hoped Poppy was on that. Then DR ABCD. Check for danger to the patient and himself, then check for responsiveness. "Sir?" He patted his cheeks, gently shook him. Nothing.

What was next? That's right. Airways. He put Mr. James on his back and tilted back his head, checking his opened mouth was clear. It was, so he moved to the next stage: breathing.

Jake looked, listened and felt for ten seconds, but Mr. James wasn't breathing, with no chest rise or fall. He pinched the soft part of the man's nose closed then breathed into the man's mouth. His chest lifted then lowered. He placed the heel of his left hand on the lower half of Mr. James's breastbone and placed his other hand on top, interlocked his fingers then used his body weight to start compressions. One, two, three, all the way up to thirty. Then two breaths. With no defibrillator handy, unless they had one in the western town or movie lot, he had to maintain this rhythm until he got a response. "Poppy!"

She limped in, still talking on the phone.

"Is there a defibrillator somewhere?" He glanced up at her.

Her eyes were huge. "I don't know."

"Where's your mom?"

"I don't know!" Her voice broke on a sob. "Don't let him die. Please, don't let him die!"

"Not my plan," he ground out. *Lord, don't let him die.*

He continued compressions and breathing, pretty sure he heard a rib crack under one of his more energetic efforts. "What's his name?"

"Derek. His name is Derek." She sniffled.

"Call your mom."

"I tried, but she's not answering!"

"Then call your sisters. Is anyone at the movie lot?"

"Cassie is, I think."

"Call Cassie then."

"Okay."

He continued his ministrations as Poppy made more phone calls, her voice pitching up and sounding slightly more hysterical with each one.

"I've called the medics, but it'll take them forever to get here."

He didn't need her getting hysterical. "Pray Poppy."

Just as his arms were getting weary, and he wondered how long to keep going, another woman rushed in. "Dad!"

"Oh, Cassie!" Poppy cried.

Cassie's arrival shoved fresh steel into his actions, her willingness to breathe for her dad giving him a chance to catch his own breath. He locked his arms for chest compressions and pretended Poppy's dad was the dummy he'd worked on during the first aid training earlier this week.

Stayin alive, stayin' alive. The tempo of that classic song matched the speed the first aid trainers had advised. Thirty more compressions. Then Cassie breathed.

"Come on, Dad," Poppy begged.

"Dad, you have to walk me down the aisle," Cassie pleaded, as Jake resumed compressions again.

"Come on, Derek. You need to wake up. Your daughters need you."

A twitch. Was that movement? He paused, and as he did, Derek coughed.

"Dad?"

Derek coughed again, and Jake rolled him onto his side into the recovery position.

"What are you doing?" Poppy asked.

"He needs space to breathe. You should probably go outside and wait for the EMT. They might find it hard to know where to go."

"But Dad—"

"Go, Poppy," Cassie said. "You being outside is the best thing that can happen."

"But—"

"Go!"

The rawness in Cassie's command drew his attention to Poppy's stricken face. She lowered her face, clutching at her crutches, her mouth a mutinous line.

If he wasn't so exhausted he would offer to go in her place. He stretched his sore fingers and caught his breath instead.

"You're going to be okay." Cassie stroked her father's head and glanced at Jake. "I don't know what to say except thank you."

He lifted a shoulder. "Glad I could help."

His chest squeezed. This must be why God had wanted him here. His skin tingled. God had wanted him here. To help save a man's life. To help save a man's *life!*

He reeled, and whether it was from that revelation or the fact he was exhausted, he moved to the sink and cupped his hand and drank some water. Splashed his face. Braced on the sink. Oh, thank God. *Thank You God.*

"Who are you?" Cassie asked.

"Jake."

Her eyebrows rose. "Poppy's Jake?"

"Yeah, no. She pretty much hates me."

"Jake the Fake she's called you."

Figured.

"Jake the Snake, too."

Wow. "The woman likes a rhyme."

"Jake the Flake, Jake the Rake—"

"I don't know what that last one is, but it's not good, is it?"

"No." She studied him, her eyes narrow. "What *are* you doing here?"

Moment of truth time. "Okay, so this will sound weird, but earlier, like an hour ago or so, I was driving past on my way home when I felt this strong need to drive here."

She raised an eyebrow.

"I didn't want to. Your sister made it pretty clear she never wanted to talk to me again, and I don't want to disrespect her boundaries."

"And yet here you are."

"Because I felt this voice say I needed to come here. I thought it was God, okay? Which is weird, I know. But that's why I came. Not because I wanted to, but because I felt like God wanted me to. That's all. Okay?"

She studied him a long moment, then her eyes filled. She shook her head.

Great. It looked like he was ticking off all the women in the James family. He probably should get out of here before Derek woke up properly and decided to deck him for making his womenfolk cry.

Jake inched back, moved to the sink, drank some more water. Then stayed out of the way as yet another female hurried in, kneeling where he had moments earlier. Then Leonie rushed in, her hands at her throat, and he figured that was his chance to escape.

They didn't need him. Derek was breathing on his own,

although that rib that might possibly be cracked was sure to be painful.

He cleared his throat. "Uh, when the EMT gets here you might need to tell them that Derek may have a cracked rib. Sorry."

Leonie glanced up at him, her brow crinkling. "Jake? What are you doing here?"

The other woman's eyes rounded. "*You're* Jake?"

Cassie affirmed. "Poppy's Jake the Snake."

"Yeah, I'm going to go now."

"Don't—"

"I'll send Poppy inside and tell the EMT where to go."

"Oh, thank you." .

"Jake?" Leonie again. "What *are* you doing here?"

Yeah, the more he told his story about what he had thought was a God prompting the less believable it sounded even to his own ears. "I'll go."

"He felt like God wanted him to stop by," Cassie announced.

"You did?" Leonie asked.

He half shrugged, took a step back.

"Oh, come here." She staggered upright then hugged him. "Thank you. Oh, thank you for obeying God. I don't know what I would've done if Derek had died."

He patted her awkwardly on the back then released her, glancing up in time to see the EMT rush in, followed by a dusty, limping Poppy. Who let out a sob at seeing her father who was now sitting partly upright, then another as she rushed to her mother's arms.

Her gaze met his for a moment, and for a moment he thought maybe he'd glimpsed gratitude, before she shuttered them and glanced away. So he walked outside, hands on head, and wondered if he still had the energy to drive nearly two hours home.

CHAPTER 9

The next hours passed in pain and confusion. Mom rode with Dad in the ambulance, while Jess drove in a little later on. Poppy, thanks to her broken leg, hadn't just been able to hop in and go too, despite her pleading.

"But we'd need to change vehicles to fit you in."

"I'll be fine!" she'd insisted. "I just want to see him. Do you know how unfair it is to feel like I can't do anything?"

Her sister sucked in an audible breath, as if trying to draw in patience. "I can understand—"

"I *hate* being left out all the time."

She winced inside. She sounded exactly as she had when she was six years old. The youngest, never included, staying behind to help her mom in the garden while the others went and did fun stuff around the ranch. The fact they were doing things like fixing fences or looking after animals that she wasn't interested in doing anyway wasn't the point. She wanted to feel included, like she was just as important as they were.

Eventually Cassie had been convinced to use her own battered truck to take Poppy in. The backseat had been laden with pillows and cushions to ease the journey, but the lack of effective suspension meant she had still found it extremely uncomfortable, her leg throbbing with fresh pain. But at least she got there.

Cassie dropped her off, wheelchair and all, which probably made a difference as she was considered by the staff to be a priority visitor, and she and Cassie were soon taken to the waiting room near Calgary Memorial's emergency department. There they found Jess, who was with Tom. He was holding her hand, their faces grim.

Panic struck. "Is he...?" She couldn't say the words. Couldn't say *that* word.

"He's alive."

A whoosh went through her soul.

"Thank You Jesus," Cassie murmured.

"Amen," Poppy whispered.

"A nurse came and got Mom, so hopefully she'll be back soon with news."

Poppy slumped into the wheelchair, hating this aching lump of leg that forbade her from doing what she really wanted and rushing in to find out what was really wrong. Impetuous wasn't her middle name, but some days it felt like it might've been. Conviction struck. Hence why she had gotten into this mess in the first place.

The doors opened, and Mom appeared, looking more worn and gray than Poppy ever recalled seeing her before. She was getting older. Growing frail. And for the first time Poppy was glad she'd been home and not two provinces away, when it might've been too late.

Her sisters rushed to Mom, while Poppy struggled to release the brake. Stupid wheelchair. Then Tom knelt and helped her. "Th-thanks."

"I'm so sorry, Poppy," he murmured. "This isn't easy for you, is it?"

"N-no." His understanding surprised her. Usually he was all

about cracking unfunny jokes. She was thankful at least someone here understood her challenges.

By now her sisters were peppering Mom with questions, having started without her, like they always did.

"Maybe Leonie would like to sit," Tom suggested.

Mom looked at him gratefully, and Jess led her right back to where they had been sitting before, meaning Poppy had to wheel herself back too. Man. Her hands slipped. She'd never realized how heavy and cumbersome these things were. Or how little muscle power she had in her upper body. How did people who weren't fit do this?

Tom came and helped her. "Hope that's okay," he said. "I don't want to overstep. I know you like to be independent, like your sisters."

"Thanks."

Why was it her sisters had lucked out with good men while she'd never been able to find a good one? But no. Now wasn't about that. Now was about finding out what was wrong with Dad.

"...so they have said he'll need to stay in the high dependency unit for several more days."

"But he'll be okay?"

"The doctor said this has weakened him considerably, but yes, he should be okay."

There were various mutterings of *Thank You Lord*, and *Praise Jesus*, then Mom was hugged by Cassie and Jess in a love sandwich. Which left Poppy on the outer, as usual.

She exchanged glances with Tom who shrugged and half smiled, like he knew his was a support role. But Poppy knew she was supposed to be one of the leading players, and yet here she was, out in the wings watching on again. Feeling like she was the understudy to her own life.

Mom then sighed, then moved to draw a hand down Poppy's hair. "Thank you all for coming."

"Franklin messaged to say he's on his way too," Jess said.

Family, coming together at a crucial time. They might have their differences, but love was what really mattered.

Cassie nodded, biting her lip. "We should postpone the wedding."

In three days' time.

Her mom's face sagged a little more, but she nodded. "I'm so sorry."

"It's not your fault. It's nobody's fault." Cassie hugged her.

"Everyone will understand." Jess glanced at Poppy.

She nodded. "That's right. They'd want Dad to be healthy, and he'd want to be there too."

Mom sighed. "He always said he couldn't wait to walk you girls down the aisle."

"We'll contact everyone, won't we?" Jess raised her eyebrows at Poppy.

"Uh, yeah, sure." She found a small smile for Cassie. "You don't need to worry."

"Thanks." Cassie's eyes shimmered.

Whoa. Her sister didn't often show emotion. Unlike Poppy, who tended to oscillate between the highs and lows of happiness and sadness.

Then she realized just what Cassie was facing. For this was far more than just postponing a wedding. With Dad out of action for weeks, probably months, Cassie's plans to step into running the ranch herself one day had just taken a mighty leap forward. Far from only having to delay a wedding a few weeks, she now had to somehow extract the knowledge of a lifetime of ranch work from her father and start applying it herself. And while she'd been learning on the job there was always a lot more to know that would only be revealed in the actual doing, and Mom would only be able to help so much. Depending on what was involved, getting married had possibly just taken a back seat to taking the reins of the ranch.

Poor Cassie. This would be so hard.

She moved her wheelchair to inch closer to Cassie and tried to give her a hug, when Harrison rushed in. "I just got your message." He hugged Cassie. "I'm so sorry."

Poppy paused, her heart twisting disconcertingly, just as her leg had when she'd fallen before. Cassie didn't need her. She had Harrison. She glanced at where Jess was talking to Tom and Mom. Jess didn't need her. She had Tom. Franklin had Hannah. Mom had Dad—and yes, praise the Lord, Mom had him still. But Poppy?

She was on the outer. A satellite circling the planets of happy relationships, knowing her heart felt just as cold and sterile as a mechanical device out in space. Her heart might work, but it wasn't alive. She might express joy, but deep within her heart remained cold and untouched.

But then, maybe God didn't want her to ever feel joy again. Why should she? Not when she had messed up the way she had.

THE STILL BLUE waters of Sylvan Lake went some way to quieting the inner turmoil he'd experienced these past few days. Time to celebrate Canada Day with his folks and brother and Sylvie, time on the lake with his dad and Ryan, made him glad for the simple ties of family. And all the more glad, knowing he'd helped keep another family together. Jake shivered. It still stunned him how easily the result could have been different.

"You okay?" Ryan asked.

"Yep."

He hadn't explained anything to them, barely able to process things let alone articulate it to others, which meant he'd earned a few concerned looks in recent days.

An unknown number flashed on his phone. He didn't answer. Then when they didn't leave a message, he shrugged. Probably a telemarketer.

He returned to fishing, then it rang again. Again.

Fine. Whoever it was obviously was in a hurry to talk.

He pressed *Accept Call* and said cautiously, "Hello?"

"Hey, it's Franklin."

"Franklin?"

"Franklin James. I hope you don't mind but I asked Ryan for your number."

"Okay. Uh, hi."

"I... I can't believe what has happened to my dad, and the fact that you were somehow here at exactly the right time to save his life. It's such a miracle. So, thank you. Thank you so much. Today was supposed to be my sister's wedding day, which obviously isn't happening. But when I think how close we were to losing Dad..." He cleared his throat. "Anyway, I'm here at the hospital and my mom and dad would like to see you to say thanks, if you think that would be okay."

Jake closed his eyes, the pungent smell of fish rising to his nostrils. "When?"

"Whenever suits you. You're a hero in our eyes and we can never thank you enough."

"I did what anyone else would've done," he said gruffly.

"Except nobody else was there to do it. Well, nobody except Poppy, and she was barely able to help."

He couldn't respond. Poppy obviously did care about her father, but Franklin was right. A broken leg meant she wasn't exactly positioned to be the most able person in a crisis.

"So, uh, is there a chance you could swing past Calgary Memorial in the next week? I know that Dad would really appreciate it. Mom too."

He closed his eyes. "I'm actually not in town at the moment. I'm fishing at Sylvan Lake with my folks."

"Oh. Okay. Well, maybe if you're heading back this way you could call in sometime soon. I certainly don't want to put you out. But if you could at all, I know it would mean a lot to them. And to the rest of us."

The 'rest of us' probably didn't include Franklin's youngest sister, who he was still fairly sure wouldn't want to see him again. "If I'm down that way in the next week I'll try to stop by."

"That'd be awesome. I really don't want you to go out of your way, but it would be great to thank you properly. I still can't…" Franklin paused. Cleared his throat again. "I still can't believe Dad was so close to dying. If you hadn't been there…"

"Like I said to your sisters, I felt this strange kind of compulsion, like God wanted me to go there, and I guess that was why."

"Yeah, but not everyone would have listened to that kind of feeling, so, thank you. You'll never know how grateful we are."

He was starting to get some idea.

"It's just wild to me that Ryan's brother is the man who stepped in. So yeah. Thanks a million. And if you are back in Calgary, it'd be awesome to shake your hand. So please, let me know if you are. This is my number, obviously." Franklin chuckled. "Anyway, I'll let you get back to your fishing. But please know that you are in our prayers. We all thank God for you."

Emotion clutched him, filling his throat, and it took several swallows before he could say, "thanks."

The call ended, but the emotion swirled on. To know that there were people who thanked God for him felt huge. And how ironic that it was the family of the woman who loathed him. He bet she wasn't thanking God for him. Or if she was, it was merely that he was in the right place at the right time.

He sank against the side of the boat, glanced at his dad whose eyebrows were raised. "Who was that?"

"Franklin James."

"Hockey guy?"

"Yeah."

Ryan glanced across. "Huh. I wondered why he wanted your number. What's he doing calling you?"

So this was fun. He hadn't actually told his family about what had happened. And now, rather than boasting, he actually felt kind of shy. "He just wanted to say thanks."

"For what?"

He exhaled. Then told them about the weird sensation to go visit, omitting the ugly part with Poppy before, except to say she was there but on crutches so couldn't help too much with her broken leg.

"Dude, you're a hero," Ryan said, with what looked like respect in his eyes. "Why didn't you say something earlier?"

Because who did that? He shrugged. "It was good when Cassie came in and started doing the breathing." He half smiled. "It's kind of weird blowing into someone's mouth you've never met before."

"I don't know. I think it'd be weird to do compressions on a woman," Ryan said.

"Apparently more women die from heart attacks because people don't want to do chest compressions on them. People are worried they'll embarrass them or something. Which is a pretty sad reason for someone to end up dead."

Ryan frowned, his head tilting. "And you know this how?"

"We had training at work on this last week." He shrugged. "Even that felt like God's good timing, getting training just before needing to use it."

"Some might call that a coincidence, but I always think it's a God-incidence," his dad said.

"It was really interesting timing." First bumping into Franklin at the gas station, then that inner prompting to take flowers and apologize, then to go again despite being asked not to. He sure hoped nobody thought he was Poppy's stalker.

"Anyway, Franklin says he and his dad want me to visit. But I don't know."

"Dude, you're a hero." Ryan punched his arm. "Of course you should go."

"I just don't want things to get awkward."

"How could things be awkward?"

Crunch time. "I, uh, once dated Franklin's youngest sister."

Ryan blinked. "*You* dated Poppy?"

"Well, yeah."

"Are you serious? Poppy James dated *you?*"

Awesome to see how little his brother regarded his dating prospects.

"And we didn't know this why?"

He shrugged. "Because it didn't end well, and she doesn't like me. Which is why it's awkward."

Ryan whistled. "Well, you might find she likes you a bit more now."

"Yeah, I don't think so."

"Well, at least the rest of her family does, so that's gotta count for something right?"

"Maybe." And maybe it would be easier if God hurried up and answered another prayer too, and removed all feelings for Poppy James from his heart.

HE DIDN'T LIKE HOSPITALS. They reminded him from when he was a kid and he had his tonsils out. He'd gotten an infection which meant a simple visit ended up lasting much longer. Not fun when he was an active kid and had to spend the summer taking care of his throat. Still, today wasn't about traipsing down memory lane, but hopefully fulfilling this request and then putting distance between himself and this family. He didn't want to be the person on the outskirts of their world, who looked like he was knocking on their door, trying to get in. He had almost reconciled himself to not being that person.

He'd texted Franklin that he was coming, and was unsurprised to see him in the foyer, his tall, broad-shouldered frame hard to miss. Several little kids were talking with him, and he was signing something. That was the celebrity world that Franklin and Ryan lived in, and he did not.

Franklin excused himself then moved to him, hand outstretched. "Jake."

"Hey."

Then Franklin ensconced him in a giant man hug, where he could literally feel the gratitude.

"I know it must seem a lot, but like I said we're all so thankful for you." Franklin eased back. "Let me take you upstairs. They shifted Dad into a private room now he has stabilized."

"That's good to hear."

They small-talked on the stairs as they walked up to the floor where Franklin's dad was resting. Jake shared about his fishing. Franklin shared about his summer plans.

"I love this city but don't love how busy it gets at this time of year."

"Same." The Calgary Stampede might be the world's biggest rodeo and bring in over a million of tourists each year, but the locals always looked forward to regaining their city and space.

He wondered if it was just the parents here now. Anyone else—okay, Poppy—he would much prefer to avoid. But asking that question felt a little pointed, so it was probably best not to.

"Okay, here we are." Franklin gestured to a corridor, and a room with an opened door. "Hey Dad, there is someone here to see you."

The room was shadowed, but Derek looked three million percent better than the last time Jake had seen him. "Hello, sir."

"Jake Guillemette." Derek held out his hand. "My hero, huh?"

"I only did what anyone else would."

"Yeah, I can't be too sure of that." He shifted, then grimaced, to his wife's concern.

Jake exchanged glances with Franklin whose expression was warmer than Jake ever recalled seeing.

"Uh, care to explain to an old man just what you were doing out in my neck of the woods?"

He explained once again, feeling less silly this time. It helped that these people were Christians and grateful, and could see with the benefit of hindsight what obedience in that moment of weird prompting had meant.

"Whew." Derek shook his head. "So you were heading home after work in Canmore and felt a God-given prompting to swing by, huh?"

"That's about it."

"I don't know what to say but thank you."

Leonie drew close and hugged him. "Thank you again for saving my husband."

He patted her on the back. "Happy I could help." Honestly, all this thanks was getting a little overwhelming. "How are you feeling, sir?"

Derek wheezed, which drew Leonie's alarmed gaze. "I'm fine, I'm fine. Don't fuss." He glanced at Jake. "The doctors tell me I'm doing a lot better now. Although I do have a busted rib."

Jake winced. "I'm really sorry about that."

"Hey, if a busted rib means I'm still alive then you've got nothing to be sorry about."

He nodded, not sure what else to say. "Have they given you a timeframe for returning to the ranch?" That was safe to ask, wasn't it?

"I think it's supposed to be in another week or so."

"But not to work," Leonie said firmly.

Derek sighed. "I feel bad that Cassie had to pause her

wedding and take on ranch responsibilities again. She shouldn't have to do that because of me."

"You know she wants to do it because of you," Leonie said. "She'd rather do the work than not have you around. You need to remember that, my dear."

Derek gave Jake a resigned-looking smile. "Have you got someone who bosses you around like this woman does me?"

"Actually, no."

"Well, I have a daughter who is still single." Derek gave Jake a wink.

Jake's mouth sagged. "Sir, I—" Had no words. This would not end well. Man. Should he admit to once dating Poppy? He peeked across at Leonie.

She bit her lip.

Okay, well, that didn't look like she thought he should say anything. Nobody needed Derek having another heart attack. Or Franklin joining him with chest pains. He had to get out of here. ASAP.

Franklin snickered. "I bet Poppy would like to know Dad is trying to set her up."

The click-thud-scrape of crutches on linoleum drew their attention to the door.

"Dad is trying to set who up?" Poppy glanced between them, before her eyes met Jake's, and widened.

Nope. He had to leave now. This would not end well at *all*.

CHAPTER 10

What was *Jake* doing here? And just what was Dad saying to him? Dad might be ill, but what she'd thought Franklin had just said sounded awfully suspicious to her. Because in that context, the only potential 'set up' involving a 'her' had to mean herself, didn't it? And while Dad had never been a romantic, he had liked seeing his other daughters find kind gentlemanly men with whom Cassie and Jess could settle down with one day. Hence, the sooner he shook loose the idea from his brain that Jake was anything like that, the better.

Jake didn't belong. He wasn't someone who was making a difference in this world. He was ordinary. He worked in a factory, for goodness sake. And call her judgy, but that wasn't exactly life changing. He'd never see his name in lights somewhere, like Harrison or Tom, like she'd dreamed of for herself. How she'd ever fallen for his charismatic schtick she didn't know. Put it down to a younger, more foolish and gullible self.

"Hi there." She kissed her mom's cheek, briefly hugged Franklin, and ignored Jake, brushing past him to her father's bedside. "Hi Dad. How are you feeling?"

"Getting better by the day." He patted her head as she bent to kiss his cheek. "But aren't you going to say hello to Jake there?"

She pointed her head in the right direction, her gaze not meeting Jake's. After the last encounter she felt a weird mix of smugness and shame. "Hi."

"Aw, come on, sis. You can do better than that. Jake is a *hero*."

"Uh, I'm really not—"

"Exactly," she agreed. "It was more a case of him being in the right place at the right time."

"Wow," Franklin muttered.

"Now don't you be like that, dismissing what God can do." Dad's face pinked.

"Poppy, your father needs to stay calm," her mom murmured in an undertone.

"I'm sorry, Dad. I didn't mean to sound dismissive. I'm glad you're okay."

"I'm only okay because of this young man." Dad pointed to Jake.

She glanced at Jake, this time meeting his eyes. This time his gaze veered away. Good. This was her family, her time with them. He shouldn't be here. He was intruding.

Except… except they wouldn't be standing here, talking with Dad if it wasn't for Jake's actions. She ducked her head, as remorse washed over her. Oh, she was a horrible person.

"Well, sir, I'd better go. I'm really glad you're on the mend. I've been praying for you, and I'll continue to pray for a full recovery."

"Much appreciated, Son."

Son?

Dad extended a hand to Jake which he accepted, then Mom hugged him, Franklin too. It was like her whole family were in a conspiracy to love the man, while she still felt so conflicted.

Okay, yes, she did appreciate him. But no, she was guarding her heart around him too. This man was dangerous for her hormones.

Even from the quick glance she had before she could see how the green of his T-shirt made his eyes sparkle a little more.

"Bye Poppy."

She nodded, offering a quick mouth contortion that might pass for a smile—if one were blind, maybe. Then she pivoted back to her dad. "So, Dad—"

"Wait a moment, Son."

Jake paused as Poppy writhed inside. Son? Again? Dad had sometimes called Harrison and Tom "Son" but he'd known them for years.

"If there's anything we can ever do for you, or if you ever need a meal, please know you're always welcome to drop by."

"Uh, thanks, but—"

"Or if you need help with that new factory of yours or anything, please don't hesitate to call. We're in your debt."

"Thanks, sir."

"It's Derek, Son."

"Thank you Derek, but I really don't want you to feel obliged. I was only doing what I thought God wanted me to. And after all He's done for me, well, let's consider it a debt I owed repaid in some small way. Partly, anyway."

Jake's eyes slid to Poppy for a fraction of a second.

Wait. Was he trying to imply this was part of what he owed *her*? That by helping her dad as he'd done he hoped it'd somehow help make up for the past? Resentment flared. She didn't think repentance worked that way.

"I should go."

Yes, you should.

Franklin extended a hand. "Thanks for coming, Jake. Really appreciate it."

"No problem. Bye."

Jake lifted a hand, and like puppets on strings her family members lifted theirs.

She kept her hands pinned to her sides, exhaling as he finally left.

"Want to sit?" Mom asked her, gesturing to a chair.

"Yes," she finally admitted. It was good to stand and not look like an invalid while around Jake, especially after sitting around so much all the time these days. But now her leg was starting to throb. Good thing Jake had left before her pride had needed to stand down and forced her to take a seat.

"So, Dad," Poppy clasped his hand. "How are you doing? Really."

"I told you. I'm fine." Dad seemed distracted. "He's a nice young man, isn't he?"

Poppy bit her lip, as Mom murmured the affirmative.

"You could do worse," Franklin teased.

"Shut up," she muttered.

"Poppy," her mom said in a reproving tone.

"What? Just because a man saves someone's life doesn't make him a hero."

"Mm, I think you'll find it kind of does," Franklin murmured.

Ugh, her brother was so annoying sometimes. "I hope Cassie gets here soon." Having Jess here would be even better. At least some members of her family knew enough to understand why Jake Guillemette was not the hero people here seemed to believe him to be.

"Where *is* that sister of yours?" Mom asked.

"Cassie dropped me off. The parking areas are crowded."

"All that celebrating by wannabe cowboys and cowgirls."

Poppy returned Franklin's smirk. People who got excited by the high of watching rodeo action at the Calgary Stampede, then after a few drinks thought they'd try out the mechanical bull riding contraptions inevitably learned that did not end well. Franklin had once had a teammate do that in the offseason who had been sidelined for months because he'd twisted a knee. He was no longer with the team.

"Speaking of a cowgirl, who is definitely not a wannabe, look who's here," Franklin said.

Relief filled her as Cassie entered. Thank goodness. Cassie had actually competed at rodeos and done pretty well before the demands of the movie set and ranch duties had set in.

"Hey, Dad. Mom, Franklin." Cassie gave hugs and kisses—probably what Poppy should have done, instead of being startled into rudeness by the sight of Jake.

"You'll never guess who I just bumped into in the hall."

"Jake Guillemette," Franklin said smugly.

"How did you—?"

"I asked him to come," Franklin said. "I knew Dad wanted to see him. To thank him."

"Thanks seems like such a hollow word," Mom murmured.

"I'm sure he understands. What can you do to ever repay someone who saves another man's life?"

"I think we should see if he could come to Cassie's wedding," Dad mused.

"What?" Poppy exclaimed. "No, you can't do that."

"Why not? We're paying for it."

Cassie glanced at Poppy. "Dad, you know Harrison offered to pay—"

"You're my daughter, so I'm paying. And I'm grateful you decided to keep it at the ranch. I don't think I'll be up for traveling any time soon."

True. There went any hope of a surprise destination wedding, as she might've overheard Harrison murmur to Cassie a time or two. Not an elopement, but a chance to go away, escape the fuss, "for you deserve time away, Cassie," Harrison had insisted.

"Isn't that what a honeymoon is for?" Cassie had countered.

"I can't wait for the honeymoon," Harrison had murmured,

seemingly forgetting Poppy had been lying in the next room, quite unable to move, quite unwilling to hear the sound of their enthusiastic kissing.

No. Her stomach wrenched. While some people might be looking forward to spending 'alone time' at last, others knew that 'alone time' pre-marriage led to regrets.

"I really don't understand this antipathy toward the man, Poppy," Dad complained now. "You act like you dislike him."

What could she say that was true yet wouldn't expose too much? She glanced at Cassie who pressed her lips together. No, she didn't want to give her dad more heart pain by admitting the cold hard facts.

"I don't know. I guess he just seems to lack ambition."

"And you know this how?"

She shrugged.

"I thought you didn't know him very well." Franklin eyed her.

"I know enough."

"Well, clearly you don't. You know he is responsible for setting up and running an engineering factory in Canmore?"

He was?

"He's Ryan's brother, and they've traveled to some interesting places over the years, like Europe."

He had? Oh. "I didn't know that."

Franklin nodded. "Exactly."

"And I can't be sorry to see my youngest daughter with a man who seems to care about others." Dad murmured.

'Seems to' having been the operative phrase in the past. How could she ever trust Jake again? Jake might act nice now, but how could she know if he really had changed?

THE QUESTION CHASED her through the rest of her visit, then all the way back home.

Dad seemed to be doing well, even if the enforced delay for the wedding had led Cassie to some interesting questions of her own.

"I just don't know what to do."

Poppy glanced at her sister as the poplars that marked the ranch's driveway came into view. "About what?"

Cassie sighed. "Do you think this is a sign that God doesn't want us to get married?"

"What? Don't be crazy. Of course God wants you two to get married."

Cassie sighed. "It just feels so weird. Your leg happens, then Dad has a heart attack, now I'm snowed under with so much stuff to do."

Guilt strummed. Here was poor Cassie with too much work while apart from some dumb exercises to strengthen her leg, Poppy was bored witless. "I can help you if you like."

"Really?"

The skeptical look Cassie threw her made her wonder just how self-centered she'd seemed. "Look, I'm sorry if I've been a little self-absorbed lately. I might not be able to do much, but if there's something I can do I'd like to help. Really."

Cassie smiled. "I've appreciated all you've done in helping rearrange things for the wedding." To a date four weeks away. The doctors had advised that Dad should be up to walking Cassie down the aisle by then.

Phoning guests to reschedule had been one way to feel like she was finally contributing.

"Well, if there's anything more I can do, please let me know. I can help with the finances for the ranch if you like. I used to do that for Bailey's dance school."

Cassie nodded. "That'd be really helpful, thanks. Numbers has never been my thing."

"And just so we're clear, I don't think that God is using a

heart attack to stop you marrying Harrison. Stuff happens. It doesn't mean it's a sign of something significant."

Cassie nodded slowly, eyeing her.

"What?"

"So what do you think about the fact that Jake just so happened to be going past and felt an urge to swing by, just as you were by yourself and unable to do anything?"

She pressed her lips together. She could argue that was a coincidence but it felt deeper than that.

"I can't get over that," Cassie murmured.

Neither could Poppy. "I know. What kind of man has the gall to go where he knows he isn't wanted?"

"That's not what I meant." Cassie stared at her. "Honestly, Poppy. He saved Dad's life. How can you be so cruel?"

Because she was in the habit of distrusting Jake Guillemette. And praising someone she'd learned to loathe felt as foreign as speaking Russian. "I *am* grateful," she insisted.

"Please." Cassie rolled her eyes. "Dad would have died if Jake hadn't been there. The doctor said that. You certainly couldn't do anything."

"I waved down the EMT."

"Well, sure, that was a big help. He would've been *dead* if Jake wasn't here."

"He's not a hero," she muttered.

"He's not the villain you painted him out to be either."

Cassie only said that because she didn't know the truth.

"No, don't look at me like that. I don't care what he did, and I suspect that if he did what I think he did, he didn't do it alone."

Her heart swooped, then began to tremble, like a bird fluttering its wings preparing to take flight. Cassie knew?

"Oh, Poppy." Cassie's face fell. "Why?"

Tears—far too quick to spring to life these days—rushed to her eyes. "I... I don't know why. We got carried away."

"He didn't rape you?" Cassie asked gently, but with a glint in her eye that resembled steel.

"No!"

Cassie pursed her lips, looking so much like a younger version of Mom for a moment that Poppy had to blink.

Shame washed over her, sending coolness rushing along her skin. Her stomach tensed then grew queasy, as if she were lost at sea. "I know it was wrong," she whispered.

"Mom and Dad don't know, do they?"

"No. And I *never* want them to find out."

"Does Franklin?"

She shivered. "I hope not."

"Fine."

"And don't go telling Harrison either."

"He doesn't need to know all of the family secrets. Anyway, I really don't think that this is something for which he'd judge you too harshly."

Because Harrison had built a bit of a reputation as a ladies' man prior to meeting Cassie, which probably meant he'd done exactly as she had, but many, many times over. No, he probably wouldn't judge.

But looking at others, comparing their sins against her own, didn't change the fact she still felt this inner coil of guilt. That she'd carried this guilt for years, ever since that night.

"I'm so ashamed." She wiped wet cheeks.

"Of what you did then or how you've been treating Jake now?"

Ouch.

"Poppy, you know how you like to give it to people straight? It's time you got your own medicine. Focusing on Jake's failings while holding onto unforgiveness is like having a log in your eye while trying to remove the speck in his."

Double ouch.

"You need to forgive him. You might think that he's done you wrong, but it sounds like you've done him wrong too.

Regardless of who's at fault, if you keep holding this in your heart, it's going to make you bitter and twisted."

Oh, she was pretty sure it already had.

"You know that unforgiveness is more about setting free the person who is holding resentment than it is about saying the other person gets a free pass."

"Yes."

"And you know the analogy of those Roman murderers who had to walk around with their victims strapped to their back. They were never free because the dead person would start to infect their bodies."

"I know that." She'd heard the story from a youth group talk long ago. How Roman citizens would die an agonizing death because they were never allowed to forget their crime.

She'd been like that. Never able to forget. Knowing she carried this weight, this burden of shame, even though she might try to hide behind sass and smiles or over-busy helpfulness—not that there'd been too much of any of that lately. It didn't matter how much she'd prayed or tried to do good things, still that curl of guilt lay lodged in her soul, like a splinter that would never be released. Her heart might've healed mostly, but it still wasn't completely whole.

Cassie studied her. "I know, and Harrison knows, how important forgiveness has been in our lives. And we don't want you—*I* don't want you, being infected by the sins of the past." Cassie hugged her. "Forgive Jake, okay?"

She dipped her head, and mumbled something that might've been an *okay*. But it was one thing to sound like she was agreeing with her sister. It was another to actually release Jake in her heart. And she didn't want to do that until she read what he'd actually written. Which she hoped now was far more than a get well card.

She limped to where she had stored the card and sank onto her bed. Then opened the white envelope, pulled out a card that displayed a photograph of a bouquet not dissimilar to what he'd given her weeks ago.

Bracing, she opened the card. It was covered in neat handwriting, unlike what she'd expected from him. Judgmental much? Apparently.

Dear Poppy.

I'm so sorry you injured your leg. I've been praying for you to heal quickly.

But I'm even more sorry for how I treated you in the past. I know I didn't live up to my godly standards, and I'm so sorry for being responsible for you lowering yours.

She winced. Was he referring to her promise to God or was this a dig at her stupid comment about his work?

She read on.

I know you accused me of being dishonest, but I promise you that I didn't know you were 22. I thought you were older.

Older? Funny how at twenty-two she had wanted to appear older. Now she resented the thought people might think her older than her years.

I know there is nothing I can say that will make things better. I can only take comfort in the fact that God forgives us. God is able to cleanse our hearts to make us like snow. I'm trying to rest in His grace, His love and forgiveness, and I pray that you will know this too.

And that one day you will forgive me. Please.

Jake.

Her eyes burned, her heart sore at his words.

Forgiveness. The word carried a far greater weight than what was suggested by a mere eleven letters.

Forgiveness. To live free or forever let resentment fester within, like an itch within her cast-bound leg that could never be satisfied.

Forgiveness. Jesus might've made the way plain by dying on a cross so all people could be reconciled to Christ, but ultimately the choice to extend it to others—to Jake—was hers.

CHAPTER 11

Jake was grateful to escape the office. Staring at a computer for so many hours was making his brain and muscles turn to mush. He needed to get out of here.

He saved his files, shut down his computer and spun back in his chair away from the desk. Dave, advising as his mentor, had always advocated for regular exercise to offset the lengthy hours sitting at a desk. And while Jake hadn't yet found a gym, a run was as good as anything to get the blood moving.

He drove home, thankful it was a quick drive, changed, guzzled water, then began a slow jog along the creek that meandered through town. Did this creek lead all the way to Derek's ranch to become one of the three creeks in its name? He wasn't sure, but the possibility that it might only underscored the connection that seemed to exist between them. Even more so now.

He wondered how Derek was doing. He didn't want to pester them with requests for updates, although Leonie had sent another message saying Jake was welcome to come by any time.

His pace picked up. He didn't think Poppy would welcome

Jake's visit, so that was an easy no. And while Poppy hadn't exactly snarled at him at the hospital, she'd made it fairly clear she didn't want anything to do with him.

His heart dipped, and he nearly stumbled over a section of uneven path. The story of his life. Getting tripped up. Stumbling, making mistakes. Except...

The clear blue skies above reminded him he was cleansed by God. No clouds marred his soul as far as God was concerned. He could either keep his eyes on the mistakes or he could trust God to take him forward. He could look down or look up and keep his eyes fixed on the Perfecter of his faith.

He dragged in air, sucked it down. *Lord, help me to keep my eyes on You. Not on me. Have Your way in me.*

Some people liked to run with earbuds. He'd never really found a pair that fit his ears. Maybe he had weirdly shaped earholes or something, but he'd gotten used to paying attention to his surroundings, to the noises outside, to the thoughts within. Filling his head with more noise meant he couldn't always hear what God might be saying. There was no internal space to listen, or to breathe. So taking time out like this was good to think, to ponder, to pray, to listen, to obey.

He passed over a wooden footbridge and onto the other side, closer to where the town's stores and main streets lay. Past Canadian Tire, then onto the main street with its stores boasting hanging baskets of flowers. It was summer, the height of prettiness, and tourists stood eating ice-cream and peering into shop windows, as if they didn't have a care in the world.

He turned into a cross street, then slowed, his breathing ragged now as he waited for traffic to clear. He obviously needed to do this more regularly. He glanced at his phone to check his run's metrics on his health app, his gaze snagging on his screensaver photo. It was a shot from the Swiss Alps from a camping trip he and Ryan had taken years ago. Back when Ryan was still pretty new to the NHL, and excited about sharing his good fortune with his family and did so by way of occasional trips overseas. These days he seemed to have settled a lot more, focused on Sylvie and their family. A pang of envy hit.

"Lord?"

A face flashed to mind. He batted it away. That was probably just his own desire, not a God-prompting. "I need discernment to tell the difference, God," he prayed, his mutter drawing gazes from people who probably thought he was off his meds. Yeah, his bright red face and mutterings probably weren't selling the professional image that Dave hoped would get the town onside.

A half-smile at an elderly lady later, the lights turned red allowing him to cross and escape along the road that ran parallel to the main street. This section of town was older, bricked buildings holding quaint details. He checked out the business offerings. Canmore Health & Wholefoods Supplies. A paper products store. Soap company. Brewing company. A marketing firm. Then Diamond Dance Studio. He slowed, stopped, steadied himself on the brickwork as he noticed a *For Sale Enquire Within* sign propped in the window.

His heart thudded. Was this a sign from God? Like, a literal sign?

He pressed his face against the glass and peered inside. It was dim, quiet, obviously closed. But the space showed an area with seats, like a waiting area, then beyond that an open room that held mirrors that reflected what light seeped around the curtained windows.

For a second he imagined Poppy here, teaching, smiling, dancing, little kids in those pink tutu things laughing with her.

A savage pain rippled through him, and he blinked hard to cast it away. He didn't want to get caught up in the whirlpool of emotion that thoughts about a future with her always provoked. It wasn't healthy for him. And until this tension between them was resolved it would always remain that way.

He gritted his teeth as grief hit him anew. She needed to forgive him, but it had to come from her. He was helpless, waiting on the sidelines for her to want to change. He exhaled. "God, I need You to help me with this. She obviously hasn't yet forgiven me, but You know she needs to, for her own sake, if nothing else. And Lord, help me wait. And if she's not the woman for me then take all thoughts of her away."

A cough drew his attention to where the elderly woman from before was staring at him.

"Uh, hi."

"Are you quite all right, young man?"

"Um, yep. Just praying."

Her eyes widened, and he took that as his cue to make his escape, dipping the brim of his Cuttrey Engineering-branded baseball cap as he muttered a "Have a good evening" and jogged back home, his thoughts awhirl with more questions.

JOGGING SOON BECAME a regular part of his day, a routine that helped him sort through the clutter of his mind while getting the necessary fitness in. And sure, jogging while others were out visiting restaurants and enjoying life made the contrast to his own lonely existence all the more apparent, but he comforted himself with the fact that this was a busy season, and a man could only do so much. He'd attended a local church last Sunday, found some guys that seemed friendly enough, telling him about a group they attended that would resume after summer. Better Man sounded like a lot of hard work, but he knew some fellowship was better than none. And here, where he could carve out his own identity instead of being known for being someone's brother, someone's son, meant he could let people know who he was but on his own terms.

He ran different paths, getting to know the thoroughfares through town. In addition to tourists there were a lot of athletes who used the nearby high altitude training sports facilities for alpine sports, so occasionally he saw people training on in-line skates. Nothing like watching a wannabe Olympian to motivate a man to get into better shape.

He ran past the main center of town, always good to avoid, seeing it was so busy, then along the parallel street that ran just behind. Where the Diamond Dance Studio was. Huh. Still for sale. He slowed, looked inside. It still looked quiet, like nobody had visited all week. And maybe they hadn't, seeing school was out and it was mid-July. How did businesses like that cope in summer? Maybe Ryan would know, seeing he was good friends with Luc, whose wife Bailey ran a studio in Winnipeg. Not that Jake cared. Too much.

But still, that stubborn vision had continued to drift through his dreams. Poppy, here, in this studio. Dancing. Happy. Doing what she'd been made to do.

He blinked.

"You again."

Huh? He peered down. The little old lady from last week.

"Uh, hello."

"I saw you here last week, didn't I?"

"Uh, yes." He gestured to the sign. "I was curious."

"Are you a dancer?"

"No. Definitely not."

"Ah."

What a random question. "Are *you* a dancer?"

She nodded. "That's my studio. I'm Martha Diamond."

Martha *Diamond*? So, not so random after all. "Jake Guillemette." He held out a hand, which she shook briefly.

"So, Jake Guillemette, humor an old lady and tell me why you're so curious if you're not a dancer."

"Oh, I have a friend who is." *Friend* felt like a stretch. But a stubborn hope persisted in believing they would be friendly again one day.

"I see."

At her intent perusal, he felt his cheeks heat. "So, you're selling, huh?"

Her little round chin dipped. "I'm getting too old to keep on with classes. Especially after my husband died last year."

"I'm sorry."

"It happens. I never know why people get upset when old people die. It's not as if any of us live forever."

He nodded. This woman might appear sweet and genteel, but obviously had a spine of steel.

"Well, if your dancer friend is ever looking to run her own studio, then this place is going cheap."

"How cheap?"

She told him, and he felt his eyes widen a little. It didn't sound that cheap to him.

Maybe she noticed his surprise, because she frowned. "That price includes a sprung floor."

"Okay." Whatever that was.

"You want to see inside?"

It felt like he was being rushed along on a wave he had no hope of controlling. "Um, I don't think so. Not right now."

"Some other day then? I'm doing a private sale. I don't trust these realtors who want to scrape a huge percentage off my profits for doing basically nothing."

"I hear you."

"Then let me give you my information." She held it out. It was a brochure for the Diamond Dance Studio, and she tapped the phone number. "If your friend is ever interested, I'd be very happy to talk."

"Do you still run classes?" he asked.

"I can't. Not with my arthritic hip, not anymore. So I'd rather sell sooner rather than later. I've had plenty of people interested in the building, but they don't realize that it's got a sprung floor."

"I'm sorry but I don't really understand what that means."

"It means it's been built so you can jump or dance on it and it has some give so it's less hard on your joints." She smiled softly. "My Herbie put it in himself forty years ago."

So selling was not just a business decision but an emotional one too. "He sounds like a good man."

"I miss him dreadfully. But I know where he is," she pointed up, "and that I'll see him one day."

He nodded. "Heaven is a great assurance for those who believe in Jesus."

"Exactly." She nodded, eyeing him. "Are you a Christian then?"

"Yes."

"Mm. Are you single?"

"I beg your pardon?"

"Are you single?" she asked more loudly, like she thought him hard of hearing.

"Uh, yes."

"So this dancer friend?"

"Is more an acquaintance really."

"I see. Well, I have a granddaughter who needs a good man."

"Oh." Oh dear. How had he gotten entangled in this? "I'm flattered, but I don't think I'm ready for that yet."

"You look like you should be. You're in your thirties, yes?"

"Uh, yes, but I just moved to the area, and I have lots of work commitments right now—"

"Pfft. All work and no play makes Jake a dull boy. And my granddaughter is smart and pretty. And a Christian, so there's that."

"Uh, thank you. But I really should be going…" He inched away.

She sighed. "If ever you change your mind, you know how to contact me."

"Thanks." Yeah, he'd never run this way again. And as soon

as he found a trash can he was dumping this pamphlet. "Have a good evening."

He turned and ran away, feeling a little like a coward, feeling a lot like he'd just avoided being swallowed by a spider. Yes, he might've felt sorry for the lady, but it didn't mean he felt sorry enough to go out with her granddaughter. That felt crazy weird.

But when he got home, he didn't throw the pamphlet out. Just smoothed out the creases, and stuck it in a kitchen drawer.

His phone buzzed with a message from Franklin. He opened it to find an invitation. To a wedding.

> We'd all love for you to come.

His nose winkled at the all. Yeah, he was pretty certain that Poppy wouldn't want him there. But if it meant he got the chance to talk with her, maybe even mention this dance studio, then maybe it would be another way of keeping the door open.

So many possibilities, yet none he was sure he wanted to explore.

"Lord?"

"Now I want you to stretch."

She gritted her teeth, following the physiotherapist's instructions. Who knew that simple stretching could make a girl sweat like this? Well, she'd known that, but hadn't anticipated sweating to this degree today. Maybe that showed just how much she'd missed exercising in recent weeks.

She tried to follow the physiotherapist's instructions, but a persistent ache refused to let her move into the correct position. Just as it had since her dad's heart attack. She knew she'd twisted it when trying to help him, and ever since then her leg had felt extra sore, but surely it shouldn't ache like this. Had she set back her healing? Nausea rose. She didn't dare think like that. She couldn't—wouldn't—even speak it aloud, in case she somehow spoke it into being. Already she was losing condition, losing her fitness. Lying around as much as she had meant she was putting on weight. She'd gone up a cup size. Anymore and she'd have no clothes left that fit her.

The session finished, and she agreed to follow orders and continue stretching. She exited, clutching her crutches, as one of those motivational posters she'd long hated stared at her on the opposite wall.

Determination. There is no trying. There is only doing or not doing.

Ugh. Once upon a time she'd believed things like that. Now, it only seemed to mock her, beckoning to remind her of all the things she couldn't do. Like stretch properly. Like walk. Like forgive.

Ugh and double ugh. Stretching physically was one thing. But stretching spiritually?

Stretching her body felt like a sign for what God wanted her to do spiritually. Yet she didn't feel like forgiving Jake. It felt like an act of faith to even contemplate forgiving him. But since that realization—okay, remembrance—that what Jesus had done was supposed to be an example for her to follow, she realized she couldn't really claim to call herself a follower of Jesus if she let unforgiveness stay in her heart.

And truth be told, she knew those actions three years ago weren't all Jake's fault. Not entirely. She had been just as much to blame. She knew that. Cassie had been right. But forgiveness felt impossible.

Thank goodness for automatic doors that allowed her to exit into Calgary's sunshine.

She glanced down the street and saw Jess straighten from where she leaned against her car.

"What are you doing?" Jess called as she hurried to Poppy. "I thought you were going to message me when you were done."

"I'm not completely helpless," she muttered.

Jess sighed, as she helped Poppy into the car. "Independent as ever, huh?"

"Yep."

Maybe that was her problem. Independence meant she sailed pretty close to selfishness sometimes. Self-reliance. Self-focus. Living in her bubble of self-importance, when maybe God was wanting to prick that bubble by forcing her to face the past and stretch into forgiveness.

Jess closed the door and moved around, leaving a precious moment for Poppy to think. And finally whisper aloud, "God, I know I should forgive Jake. But I really don't want to." She winced. How selfish did that make her? "I'm sorry. I really need Your help to forgive him."

There was no great internal gust of wind but the next time she heard Jake's name mentioned—that night when Dad said he'd asked Franklin to invite Jake to the wedding—her reluctance to face him was less than usual. Because it was true. They needed to talk, once and for all. And even though she really didn't want to, and confrontation was not her middle name, Cassie had been right. She couldn't keep carrying this lump of shame on her shoulders. And while it felt impossible to ever fully be free of this guilt, the fact that faith said it was possible meant that maybe one day she would. But that would only likely come about from meeting Jake again. Face to face. She cringed.

ONE DAY, after she'd just completed her stretches, just prior to helping Cassie with the bookwork for the day, she glanced up and saw a car pitching dust along the driveway.

"Mom? Do you know who that is?"

Her mom joined her at the window. Dad was home, and the hours of care were taking a toll. "I didn't think the nurse was coming to check on your father until later."

The car parked, then a slender person exited, holding a bunch of flowers. Poppy's heart leaped, and she hopped her way to the front door. "Bailey?"

"Surprise!" Bailey beamed, and handed the bouquets—there were two—to Poppy, then one to her mom. "Hello, Leonie."

"Oh, Bailey." Mom wrapped her in a hug. "It's so good to see you."

"How is Derek?"

"He's on the mend. Taking things easy. Are you able to stay for a while? I can make tea."

"Thank you, I'd love that."

"Is Luc with you?"

"He's in Calgary with Franklin. He had an interview with Hannah as part of a new series she's doing on various captains in the NHL. I didn't think I could get away but turns out I could, so we're having a little getaway."

"How nice for you both."

Bailey smiled, accepted the tea. "Franklin said for me to drive out here, so I hope that's okay."

"Of course. We've got so much to catch up on."

After Bailey popped in to see Poppy's dad, they settled in to have a chat. It didn't take long in their catch up until Poppy noticed Bailey's frequent touches of her belly, which along with a certain glow, made her wonder if she was about to spill certain news like Franklin and Hannah had shared on Sunday. The family's excitement at the addition to a new family member in the New Year, providing a welcome bright note to recent events, had seen Hannah and Franklin apologize for keeping the secret.

"But we wanted to make sure this one was healthy, and then

didn't want to detract from Cassie's wedding, and then there's been a bit going on lately," Franklin had said.

They'd been swamped with hugs and congratulations and "We're all so thrilled for you both!" And Poppy had seen a softness in Hannah's features she hadn't seen before.

A similar softness she recognized in Bailey now.

"Bails, have you got something in particular to tell me?"

Bailey beamed. "We're expecting a baby!"

"Oh!" Envy panged, then she immediately quashed it by stretching to give Bailey a hug. "I'm so happy for you."

"Thanks. We're excited. It's a little sooner than we thought, but it's like a little miracle."

"It *is* a little miracle."

"So, what does that mean for the studio? For *Dance Off*?"

"Well, *Dance Off* is easy—I'll just have to say no to next year. And that's okay. I feel like if that's all the seasons I have then I'm okay with that. But the studio..." She bit her lip. Glanced at Poppy. "I have some new teachers, but I'm not quite sure what to do."

"I could come back," she offered. She loved Bails, but really would prefer not to. Not that she wanted her to think she was reluctant. Even if it was true.

"I know that we're partners, but I also don't want you to feel obliged to drop everything just to come at my beck and call."

"I think technically I'm still considered one of the dance teachers."

"Of *course* you are. But I know I've leaned on you a lot in the past few years."

She nodded. "And it's been fun. My time teaching at the Calgary studio wasn't nearly as rewarding."

"But is that all you want to do in life?" Bailey asked. "This thing with your dad made me realize that you might prefer to be somewhere closer to home. Family is forever."

"Until it's not."

"Exactly. Luc's mom is still cancer-free, praise God, but she's all the way over in Quebec, so if anything was to happen, it would take hours for us to get there. I'm so grateful to have my own family nearby, but I'm realizing that life gets a little complicated."

Sure did. And that was without adding any complicating factor of her own, such as deliberately not following God's ways. "What is it you're saying?" Poppy asked. "Don't you want me to teach anymore?"

"I'm saying," Bailey grasped Poppy's hands. "I'm saying that I want you to ask God what He wants from your life, and not to feel obliged to support me or think you need to prop up my dance studio. Not if you have dreams for something else."

"I don't."

"Maybe not right now, but you might one day. Especially if you, you know, pray about it." She smirked.

"Look who's getting sassy, Mama Bear."

Bailey grinned, delight suffusing her face. "I still can't believe it."

"Do you want a boy or a girl?"

"I don't mind."

"I bet Luc wants a boy, huh?"

"I think he'd actually like a little girl. Can't you just see him teaching a tiny pink-dressed thing to skate?"

Oh, she could. "That would be so adorable."

Someone else who'd be equally adorable as a daddy would be Franklin. There was something about big tough men who seemed to melt as far as their women were concerned. She bet that would be multiplied one hundred times if it came to a little girl.

Her mind flicked to another man, and she wondered what he'd be like as a father. These days he seemed to have patience and self-control working pretty well, at least. Far more than she did, anyway.

"So, what do you think? Would you like to come back once you're all better? Or would you maybe like to open your own studio one day?"

Her heart thumped. Her *own* studio? She'd never really thought much about that as a possibility. She was just the girl who liked to dance, who loved to perform. Sure she'd helped Bailey with some of the books and administration and even thought a few times about how she'd do things differently. But she'd always known the studio was Bailey's baby, so to speak. The buck ultimately stopped with Bailey. But if Poppy opened her *own* studio, she could run the dance classes she wanted. Ballet, tap, jazz, hip-hop, even cheer—

No. What was she thinking? If she ran her own studio there was no way she'd *ever* have the opportunity to join a national touring group. Not that she'd necessarily get in, even if her audition was flawless, as there were so many other factors involved. But now, having had more time to think about it, she realized that saying yes to one thing meant saying no to other opportunities. And what exactly would the touring nature of a dance troupe mean? Sure, she'd see the world, but she'd also seen the toll Bailey's *Dance Off* commitments had taken, like weeks of not seeing her husband. And while she didn't have a husband, or even a boyfriend, how could she develop a relationship even if she did find a suitable guy? Nobody could deny the challenges of a long distance relationship.

And what about her own family? Spending as much time at home as she had, she'd come to appreciate all kinds of things, like having her mom nearby, being able to help with Dad, even having insights into the lives of her sisters. She loved her family, loved the security of having them near. But if she joined a dance troupe that was travelling half the year, she'd lose all that. Just when she'd rediscovered how good it was to have family nearby. Dad and Mom were getting older. What would have happened if she hadn't been here and Dad had died? Or if she'd been a continent or several plane trips away? Joining a touring dance group now held less appeal than she'd figured. There were so many factors to consider.

"I'll have to think about it."

"And pray about it," Bailey urged.

"Of course."

Bailey studied her. "You seem different."

"How so?"

"I don't know. But maybe like you're more at peace."

"I have been praying more, and reading my Bible. But I think it's more that I've actually been trying to trust God while before I was trying to do my own thing."

Like holding people's sins against them. Nothing like being told she had a log in her eye. 'Doing her own thing' was another one of those oxymorons for a Christian, someone who was supposed to follow God and His prompting, rather than selfishly following her own inclinations.

Her thoughts veered again to somebody who *had* followed God's prompting, resulting in a saved life. Now she thought about it, without peering through the glasses of resentment, she could see how brave Jake had been to follow God's leading to a place he would've known she hadn't wanted him to visit again. She might've thought the man was weak, but that decision to follow God, even though he would've known he'd face her scorn, had proved he was courageous.

"I'll be praying for you," Bailey said. "Most of all that this leg of yours heals as it should. And quickly."

"Thanks, Bails."

"Anytime, Poppy."

They hugged, as fresh ease flowed. Maybe some things could work out after all.

"You're telling me it's been hurting for several weeks?"

Her heart hammered as the doctor frowned. He'd murmured his concern that it wasn't healing properly, and sent her off for a scan after she'd been forced to admit what had happened when her father's heart attack had seen her fall and twist her leg.

Her mom had gasped. "Poppy, why didn't you mention this before?"

"Because I didn't want people worrying about me when Dad was the one who needed attention."

"Oh honey, I wish you'd told us sooner. I can't believe you've been in so much pain."

"Dad was more important."

"But honey, you need your leg to work properly."

"It really would have been better if you'd let us know straightaway," the doctor said.

Poppy pressed her lips together. See? She couldn't get anything right.

The doctor looked up from the X-rays and eyed her seriously. "I'm really sorry Poppy, but this latest scan suggests that unless things improve dramatically, we'll need to re-break your leg."

Her chest tightened. No. No way. "Re-break it?"

"I'm afraid that if we don't do this surgery, you're going to always walk with the limp and certainly won't be able to dance again."

Not ever dance again? He had to be joking. "I *have* to dance," she insisted. Dancing was who she was. It was part of her DNA. And all she was good at. Who would she be if she couldn't dance? "I can't imagine not being able to dance. That would kill me."

"I know this is a lot to take in, but I think it's better to prepare yourself and know all the options rather than expect it will be fine and then be devastated if it doesn't heal."

She could appreciate the pragmatic nature of that, but it still felt really raw.

She glanced at her mom, and the emotion in her mom's face spurred hers.

And big tears escaped as she faced the certainty of a future she didn't want.

How could God do this to her?

CHAPTER 12

Jake tugged at his bow tie, loosening the fabric just a touch as the guests filled the little white church. He still didn't really know why he had agreed to doing this. Well, he did, but didn't dare think about it too often, in case it lodged in his brain then accidentally spilled from his mouth.

No. He was here because Derek had asked him. The fact that Poppy would be here was simply a bonus. And while their last encounter had felt miles better than anything in the previous three years, he still didn't feel as comfortable as he would like around her.

So he was keeping to the edges. He'd shaken hands with Franklin, met the groom who clapped his shoulder like they were best buds, which had felt so weird. Harrison Woods, a movie star he'd seen a few times on the big screen, acting like Jake was his friend. But that's what actors did, right? Acted. Jake wouldn't buy into that too much. But a few other strangers also seemed to know about him. At least they did when he gave his name.

"Oh, you're the one who saved Derek's life! Oh, he and Leonie have mentioned what you did. God bless you."

He didn't think he'd ever received so many uttered blessings as he had in the past fifteen minutes.

He glanced around where he sat in the church's wooden pew, right up the back, not wanting Poppy to see him. He was here at Derek's request, not hers. He nodded to a few others he recognized. Ainsley Beckett, Harrison's co-star, sat with Zac Parotti, one of Ryan's hockey friends. Lincoln Cash, another Hollywood icon, sat with a woman he'd overheard whispered was his wife. Other Hollywood actors and sporting legends—Mike and Bree Vaughan were here too—and family and associates, all here at the ranch's western town movie set church, a real one, apparently. And then there was little ol' him.

The music filled the room and the congregation stood, turning to watch as Jess entered, accompanied by her boyfriend Tom. Who would Poppy enter with?

The congregation pivoted as she finally entered the room. Dressed in pink, her blonde hair cascading around her shoulders, she was limping, but her smile was wide as she clutched Franklin's arm. An internal heart knot loosened a fraction. She was with her brother, no mystery guy.

He barely paid attention as the bride entered, only noting how much healthier Derek looked than the last time he'd seen him. His attention swiveled to watch the front as the slow procession continued. There were lots of slow processions today, thanks to Poppy's injured leg and her father's injured heart.

Jake's heart clenched at the bridegroom's expression, at the way he wiped his eyes.

Harrison might play a tough guy in the movies, but love for Cassie had apparently made him softer than a marshmallow. From what he knew, Harrison didn't have much family, so marrying into the James family was like gaining a family of his own. No wonder he was emotional.

The minister welcomed them, the congregation sang a song,

then they were invited to sit. Jake sat, but Poppy remained standing, leaning on a crutch he hadn't noticed before. So beautiful. She glanced out, her gaze sweeping the congregation. He lowered in his seat. He didn't want her feeling like he'd spoiled the ceremony by being there. And he'd do his best to ensure she enjoyed the day. By staying far away.

LATER, he snagged a drink and entered the big white tent where the reception was being held. Conversations fluttered around him, tables set with flowers in a rustic cowboy theme drawing his smile. A break in one of the groups huddled around talking showed a blonde, still wearing her bridesmaid gown, inundated with people wanting to talk to her. Which meant he'd stay back.

Leonie passed then paused. "Jake, I'm so glad you could come. Thank you."

"Thank you for having me."

She smiled at him. "You certainly look very nice."

"Thanks." He tugged at his collar again. "I feel like a bit of a fraud though."

"You know we all want you here."

He was pretty sure that 'all' still didn't include Poppy. He forced his gaze away from her. "Cassie and Harrison look happy." Harrison was holding Cassie in a slow waltz, as other couples danced around them. "It was good to see Derek got to dance with her."

"That was very special," Leonie agreed. "He's taking it very easy today, which is just as well. I don't want to ever again go through those awful hours when we weren't sure if he'd live."

He offered a comforting squeeze on her arm.

She patted it. "To think he nearly didn't make it."

"But he did. He's strong. Just like you all are."

"You're kind." She peered at the dancers. Then sighed. "Poor thing."

He followed to where she looked. Saw Poppy gazing wistfully at the dancing.

Of course. The dancer would want to be out dancing.

"I don't suppose you feel like being a hero again?" Leonie murmured.

"How so?"

"Poppy. I know she's been disappointed to not have the bridesmaid experience she was hoping for. And I really would love to see her dance."

"You want me to find a partner for her?"

"Would… oh, I know this is a lot to ask, but would *you* ask her to dance?"

His throat dried. "Leonie."

She shook her head. "I know. That's asking too much."

"There are a lot of men here. I'm sure plenty of them would be very happy to dance with her."

"Meaning you're not?"

"Meaning I don't think she'd be very happy to dance with me," he confessed.

"Oh, I think you underestimate yourself."

He shook his head.

"Jake, look, I know you two dated before, and it didn't end well. You told me that much. And I'm going to guess that there were other factors as well that have contributed to this angst."

His cheeks heated. This was not the kind of conversation he expected to have with Poppy's mother, especially today of all days.

"I have tried to tell her how sorry I am."

"And I think she's now taking more responsibility for her own contribution to that state of affairs. No, don't tell me. I don't want to know the details."

Good, because he had zero inclination to share.

"But if you asked her to dance I think it would help her feel like she can do things again, especially with all this uncertainty about her leg."

"What uncertainty?"

"You haven't heard? The doctor is concerned it's not healing properly."

His heart panged. "I didn't know. That's awful."

"Exactly. And she's trying to be brave, but I think it would mean a lot for her to actually get on the dancefloor and feel like that part of her life isn't over. No matter what a doctor's report might say. Can you see why I'd love for you to be a hero again?"

His lips twisted. "I appreciate what you're trying to do for her, but I still don't think she'd ever want to dance with me."

"Please?"

He sighed. What was he going to do when the mother of the bride—and of the woman he'd never fully gotten over—looked at him like that? "Fine. But I don't mind admitting that I feel like I've just been manipulated."

Fortunately, she laughed. "I prefer to think of it as strong encouragement and motivation."

"I'd prefer to think of it that way too, if I were you."

She laughed again, drawing Hannah and Franklin's interest. Franklin was cradling his wife, his hands on her stomach. Huh. So they were in the family way too.

"What's so funny, Mom?" Franklin asked.

"Oh, nothing. I'm just enjoying spending time with Jake here. He's about to go and be a hero again."

"A hero? How so?" Hannah asked, leaning back in her husband's arms.

"He's about to ask Poppy to dance."

"That does take a brave man. She's been batting them away left, right, and center," Franklin said.

Leonie patted Jake's arm. "Well, she's not about to bat you away. Just go over there and ask."

"You want her dancing?" Franklin asked.

"Of course she does," Hannah said softly. "Poppy needs to remember that all is not lost."

"Exactly," Leonie's eyes glinted. Then she looked at Jake. "Thank you."

So he braced within and went to the woman who'd openly loathed him to ask if she would like to dance.

OH, this was so hard. How could she have thought that coming to a wedding reception but not dance would be something she was fine with? She wasn't fine. She wasn't coping. Sure she might be wearing a bright red lipsticked smile, but she wasn't feeling it. Not one bit. And while a bunch of people had asked if there was anything they could do, the one thing she wanted to do she couldn't. Maybe they all knew that was a hopeless case and didn't dare ask her to dance with them.

A figure moved into view. She swallowed. Jake Guillemette sure knew how to wear a suit well. He looked as fine as he had that night when they met at the Calgary play.

His gaze met hers, and his mouth lifted on one side, like he was wryly aware of the awkwardness of him approaching her.

Her own lips tweaked upward, and he nodded, as if assured. Then, seconds later, he was standing in front of her. "Hello Poppy."

For a second, she felt breathless. "Hi Jake." She coughed, forcing air into her lungs. "You look nice."

"You look beautiful."

Her stomach twirled with his praise. But awkwardness meant she couldn't merely accept a compliment. She had to deflect. She stuck out her leg. "I'm all strapped up and nowhere to go."

"What about on the dancefloor?"

She blinked. "Are you... are you asking me to dance?"

"If you'd like. I understand you might not want to, though. But just in case you do..." He shrugged.

She glanced over to where her mom was watching. "Did my mother ask you to do this?"

"Yes."

No hesitation, like he didn't care if she didn't like his answer. But then, that was something that impressed her about him. He didn't seem to want to impress her. He simply was himself. Take it or leave it. And three years ago, she'd certainly taken and helped herself. Until she'd realized that the man he'd presented her with wasn't the real deal.

"Thanks for offering, but you can tell my mother no, I won't dance, because my leg is strapped. Remember?"

"What about if we take it really easy, really slow?"

"Like we should've done back when we were dating?"

His lips pressed together, then his chin dipped. He stepped back. "Okay."

He turned, as if to walk away, then she reached out a hand and clutched his jacket. "Don't go."

He peered back at her. "You want me to stay?"

"For a moment. I don't want Mom to feel like she needs to come over and make me happy. If you stay a moment longer than she'll think we're getting on and it's okay."

"Aren't we getting on? I thought we were."

She bit her lip. His eyes were intent on hers. His eyebrows raised, a silent question.

"Yes," she whispered.

His brow smoothed. "You know your family love you, don't you?"

"I know."

"They just want to see you happy. And I imagine it's frustrating to not dance here at your sister's wedding the way you probably want to. But right now, it's not about showing off your fancy dance moves. The thing that would mean the most to your sister and your parents now is for you to look like you're having fun."

"I *am* having fun."

"Are you?"

Well, no. Well, no she *hadn't* been, until he'd come along and started speaking to her.

"So…" He held out his hand. "Will you dance with me?"

She eyed his hand. "Are you asking because my mother asked you to or because you want to?"

"I'm asking you because I want to dance with you, Poppy."

"But my leg—"

"We'll only do what you are comfortable doing, so we'll go really slow. Okay?"

"Okay," she whispered.

She touched his hand, felt tingles rush along her skin. Then he gently, slowly walked with her to the outer edge of the dancefloor where there were less people. It was a slow song., which was just as well because the only movement she could offer him was a slight sway.

He drew her near, gently holding her hand, his other on her waist. "Is that okay?"

His breath whispered along her ear. She nodded.

Her leg didn't ache nearly as much as when she'd been forced to keep it in the same position. Rather, she was more focused on the feel of her hand in his, his hand on her waist, the way his fingers gently rested on the satin folds of her dress, never straying.

"Don't look now, but your mom is smiling."

Naturally she had to look. She peeked across, saw Mom smiling, Dad's grin, and Hannah and Cassie in near identical poses, with their hands clasped over their chests. She wrinkled her nose at them and looked the other way.

Of course, the other way meant becoming more aware of Jake's chin, the firmness of his jaw, his scent of spice and sea-salt.

She closed her eyes. Okay, so perhaps she was here because of a pity invitation, and they were barely dancing, more like swaying from side to side. But at least she was dancing. Like she was finally doing what she was made to do. Like this was what she was meant to do. And not just dance, but be with him. Be with *Jake*. She shivered.

He bent a little closer. "Are you cold?"

"No." His presence made her warm. Or maybe that was the effect of the butterflies flapping wildly inside. Was she this starved for a man's attention that she instantly felt the sense of connection with the first man who was brave enough to ask her to dance?

Or was it more that it was *this* man, a man she knew intimately well, who apparently still possessed the power to make her body flame?

"You know your family love you," he murmured, "not because of what you do but because you are theirs."

"I know."

"You do?"

She nodded.

"And if you were never to dance again, they would still love you."

"Yes," she whispered. She knew that.

"I think it's the same with God too. He loves us. He doesn't need us to do anything for Him. Even the things we think are our gifts and talents have only been given to us by God. I don't think God needs us to use them."

"But what about being a good and faithful servant? Being a good steward? You know, like those people mentioned in the Bible who are given talents and don't use them."

"What about when Jesus says I no longer call you servants, I call you friends?"

Huh. "You know your Bible better than you used to."

"I would hope so. I wasn't exactly walking with God too closely back then."

Whereas she had called herself a Christian, but done her own thing anyway. And look where that had got her. Years of recrimination and resentment. Years of regret.

She lifted her head, studied him. "I am sorry."

"For what? Dancing too slow? I gotta tell you this is about my speed."

Her mouth curved. She appreciated his attempt at humor. "No. I'm sorry for blaming you about all that stuff before. I know I was a hypocrite. That I shouldn't have blamed you. I... I'm sorry."

He drew her a little nearer, his smile, his eyes growing a little more tender. "I forgive you."

His words were like balm in her heart. The jagged edges within soothed with sweet restorative honey. Emotion rushed to spill, forcing her to sniff and blink hard.

He bent a little lower. "Are you okay?"

She was about to nod, to deny anything was wrong, when she realized this was what she'd always done. Suppress things. Deny truth. And just like she'd once needed to encourage Bailey to be honest and speak up with her family, so she needed to do the same. Fear lived in lies. Shame hid in the darkness. But confronting things and bringing things into the open allowed the spotlight of God's love to shine and caused things to be seen and addressed correctly.

She peeked up. Then across. Saw they were being watched by dozens of way-too-interested faces. She glanced back at him. "Would you mind if we went outside?"

"Uh, sure."

He held out his arm, and she grasped it, fanning herself as if she was too warm. More fakeness, but at least it gave a solid excuse for why she was leaving.

Jess drew near. "Do you need a drink?"

He paused. "Poppy?"

"No. Thanks." She needed to leave, to finally talk to him and get things said that should've been spoken about years ago. And it felt like any distractions would kill off this budding chance of reconciliation.

Jess nodded, then winked. Then glanced at Jake. "Don't do anything you shouldn't."

His cheeks flushed. He glanced down.

"Oh, I was joking." Jess grinned. "Actually, I'm not joking, but you know what I mean."

It was clear from Jake's expression he didn't know how to take that.

"She doesn't know," Poppy murmured, as soon as Jess moved beyond earshot.

"Who does?"

"Cassie. I think Mom has guessed. I don't think she's told Dad yet."

He winced. "I feel like such a fake."

"Why? You're the hero who can do no wrong, remember?"

"Yeah, we both know that's not true."

Her heart ached. Had her snide comments hurt him so that he thought that too? Or had it only reinforced what he thought about himself already?

She gestured to a couple of Muskoka chairs, positioned under a string of fairy lights that cast a warm glow, and he gently steered her in that direction. He helped her to sit, the split in her dress allowing her braced leg to prop out.

The night air was cooler, away from the noise, away from the attention, the sky a sprinkle of stars scattered among the velvet black. So beautiful. A reminder that God was the creator of beauty. She closed her eyes, noticing the insect sounds, a bird call, a frog's low, persistent croak.

"So…"

Her eyes opened, and she glanced across. He was watching her. "So." She braced.

"Did you just want air, or did you want to talk?"

Oh, how easy it would be to deny the latter. But she'd denied things for too long, and instead had let worry and speculation, anger and frustration hold sway in her heart. It was time to finally get some answers. It was time to get the truth.

CHAPTER 13

All Jake's concerns about attending a wedding when he barely knew the bride or groom had faded, his focus pinpointing to this moment. Far from being ticked off with him like he'd assumed, Poppy had been aloof at first, but surprisingly accepting. Maybe God had heard his prayers and was working in her heart too.

He'd been amazed that she had agreed to dance with him. Amazed she'd agreed to come out here too. And now, sitting here, waiting for her to spill whatever she was going to say from those perfect pink lips, he found himself itchy with anticipation.

Would she finally be honest and talk about the past? Or would she tell him to leave and never bother her again?

But he knew they had to talk, that this was an important conversation. A necessary conversation. Since her, he'd never dated again. His experience with Poppy James had scarred him, some might say scared him, and despite his attempts to project a carefree persona that wasn't interested in a long term relationship, the truth was he'd never wanted to date again, because he couldn't trust himself with a woman. So yes, he might talk a big game, but God knew that he'd never kissed a woman in three years, let alone even dared contemplate anything else. Not when the truth of what he'd done had seared his soul. Not while this woman hated him still. He'd only ever date someone else once this woman had released him from the debt he owed her. Saving her dad didn't really count.

In some ways he felt like she was supposed to be his, but he wasn't sure if that just was creepy, so he'd never speak that aloud. All he knew was that Poppy James felt bound to him in some way, and until she said they could only ever be friends, then he was still hoping for the miracle of miracles that she might one day want a redemption round with him. But that felt next to impossible, even if he was trying to be a man of faith. Especially when he knew she could do so much better than him.

She glanced at him, biting her lip. A bottom lip he'd once kissed and tasted and enjoyed. He blinked. *Lord, please take those memories away.* A prayer he must've prayed hundreds of times in the past three years.

Clearly she was nervous. But equally clearly she wanted to say something. It would probably help to start with something easy.

"The stars sure look big out here." He inwardly cringed. He was so lame at this.

She half-smiled, tilting her head to study the heavens.

The heavens. Heavens that declared the glory of God. Heavens that were mentioned in a verse somewhere in the Bible about how his sins had been cast as far away as the east was from the west.

Okay, so there was a better conversation point. "How far do you think it is to get to the east from the west?"

She peered at him. "I'm sorry?"

"You know. That verse in Psalms about how God has forgiven us that much."

"As far as the east is from the west." She tipped back her head, looking above. "It's forever, isn't it? It's been a few years since I've studied geography but from what I remember at school, there's no fixed point where east meets west, is there?"

"Which is kind of comforting, when you think about forgiveness in terms of that verse."

"True."

Silence fell between them again. Beyond, the sounds of reception music and laughter underscored the tension that lay between them. *Lord, give me wisdom. Please turn this conversation around for good. I feel so clueless, like I open my mouth and bombs keep hurtling out. Please heal this situation between us.*

Forgiveness felt like an almost tangible thing. He knew God had forgiven him, but now he wanted—needed—to hear her forgiveness too. But how to ask for that without making her feel manipulated into offering something she didn't wish to do he didn't know. *Lord?*

"Thank you for sitting here with me."

She glanced at him again. Wet her lip.

He braced, recognizing that as something she did when she was nervous. Alright then. Here we go. "Poppy, what is it you wanted to say?"

POPPY WET HER LIP AGAIN. Saw his gaze flick to her mouth then instantly back up. But despite her heart flutters at his interest she knew she had to be careful. To say what actually needed to be said.

"Why did you break up with me?" she whispered.

He pressed his lips together for a moment, then sighed. "I knew what we did was wrong and I felt ashamed. I might not have been following God too well, but I knew better. And I felt like, I felt like I had taken advantage of you."

She swallowed. Knew she had to confess this. It wasn't fair that he took the blame. "I... I had been following God, but I wanted to do that too."

He shook his head. "I still felt so bad. And then when I discovered how young you were—I thought you were older, honestly I did."

"People have always said that about me, that I look older than my age. Which will be great when I'm thirty and they think I'm two decades older."

"I can't see that happening. People will always see how pretty you are."

Some of the tension within melted at his words.

His half-smile faded. "Anyway, I felt so guilty, like I'd taken advantage of your innocence, and I knew it wasn't fair to you. Especially not when you obviously had big dreams and goals and I couldn't offer any of those things."

Just like what she'd imagined. Remorse struck anew. "You thought we were too different."

"We still are too different."

She glanced up at him. "Are we?"

He stared at her, his dark gaze seeming to sink into her bones. Just as it had before. And in that moment he subtly altered from being Jake-to-be-kept-at-a-distance, to Jake, whom she wanted to know more.

Jake, who was listening to God. Jake, who had traveled to Europe. Jake, who had hopes and dreams. Jake, who would always be older than her, but now three years had passed, thirty-three and twenty-five seemed better than thirty and twenty-two. And soon it would be thirty-six and twenty-eight. Forty and thirty-two. Age differences didn't matter so much as one aged.

Again, she was reminded how Bailey's father had balked at Bailey dating Luc, who was six years older. It seemed so silly now, but obviously had felt like such a big deal to Bailey's dad.

Time passed, things changed. Opinions changed. People changed. And it seemed like the man who sat with her now was very different to the one she'd known three years ago.

Which begged the question: who was he now? Really?

He studied her, his eyes asking questions she wasn't sure she knew how to answer. She'd tried to move on. Had tried to date other men. Had even investigated the Dream Match dating app. But it seemed her unresolved issues with Jake had always held her back from saying yes to a second date.

"What is it, Poppy?"

She swallowed again, unsure how to ask this next question.

"Poppy, what did you mean by saying 'Are we?' just now? Forgive me if this sounds crazy but it sounded like you wondered if we could really put all the past behind us once and for all."

Put the past behind her? Not hold this against him anymore? Oh, it sounded so simple to say "just forgive!" But it wasn't a case of saying magic words and expecting an immediate attitude change accompanied by lollipops falling from the sky. She knew forgiveness was harder than this. Demanded grit as much as it did to first stand en pointe. Yet forgiveness also wasn't based on her feelings, but could be an act of faith. She could rationalize things forever, but sooner or later she had to bite the bullet and will it so.

"I think we can," she finally said. "I... I think we need to."

He nodded, eyes searching hers. "Does this mean you forgive me?"

Forgive him? *Lord, help me forgive.* Crunch time. If she called herself a believer, it was time to stretch her faith to follow one of her Lord's commands. "I do," she whispered.

"You forgive me?"

She glanced up. Looked deep into his eyes. "I forgive you, Jake."

His eyes lit, and as he smiled, a wave of happiness rolled over her, like rushing water that cleansed a heart of debris. She felt free. There was power in actually speaking those words aloud.

For so long she'd felt trapped by her regrets and shame, not wanting to revisit one of the most painful moments of her life. But what if she'd been bolder, more courageous, and spoken of it then? Now she thought about it, she could have. She could've tracked him down on social media, could've messaged him again. Could've reached out, instead of focusing inwards, letting her doubts spiral, her guilt weaving around her until she was caught in a sticky web of shame, that no amount of prayers had ever been able to disentangle.

"Thank you," he murmured. "I… I've hated myself because of what I did to you."

"I hated myself because of what I did to you."

"We make a real good pair, huh?"

"The worst," she agreed. Then when his eyes widened, she realized how her words could be taken. "I mean, we've both hated ourselves for so long, and that's not good, is it?"

His lips pursed. "Maybe we should agree to let it rest in the past."

"I've heard that's what forgiveness is supposed to be like." She mentioned Cassie's recent reminder about the Roman murderers with their victims strapped to their backs.

He dipped his chin. "That's what I've felt like too. Never free. Always carrying around regret." He glanced at her. "I wish I had talked to you sooner."

She shook her head. "I don't think I would've been in any position to hear what you might want to say. But hey, the past is the past. We can't change it, we can only learn from it."

"Amen."

A bird call's floated over the hum of music and laughter. Cassie and Harrison were enjoying themselves. And after all the angst of recent months, it felt good to feel a little more able to finally relax. Which might have something to do with this much-needed conversation she'd finally had. *Hey God, thank You.*

Benji trotted by, placed his head on her lap. She rubbed him, her fingers accidentally brushing Jake's, resulting in his awkward laugh.

"Sorry."

"It's okay," she assured.

"I wish we could have a do-over," he murmured.

"Me too." To have met him without any of this angst and pain.

"So, what do you say about letting all that go and starting over?" He held out a hand. "Hi. My name is Jake Guillemette."

She grasped his hand. "Poppy James."

"It's a pleasure to meet you."

"You too."

"So, what is it you do, Poppy?"

A wry chuckle escaped. "An excellent question. At the moment, not very much. But I'm a dancer."

"No way! I looked at you and that's immediately what I thought you must be."

She chuckled. "You don't have to pretend so much."

"I asked simply because I want you to now ask me."

"Fine. What is it that you do, Jake?"

"I am about to open the Canmore branch of the Cuttrey Engineering company."

"Wow. What does that involve?"

Over the next minutes as he shared a little about what he was doing, and what his role involved, she found herself growing interested. Far from being a mere factory worker, he had a real position of authority, and was obviously a key component of a company that was considered one of the most important in the province.

"So you're important, huh?"

He shrugged. "I'll never think of myself like that."

Humble, too. "But it doesn't change the fact that you have a lot of responsibility."

"Responsibility that means I'm working harder than I have in my life. Which is why it's been so nice to come here tonight and not have to think about that at all." He shifted in his seat. "But enough about me. I want to hear about you. What have you been doing and what are your plans for the future?"

She shared about taking Bailey's classes in Winnipeg for the past two years. "She's done so well on *Dance Off Canada* that I was really happy to help her out. I was working in Calgary at a dance studio before that, but obviously I've had to give up teaching dance for a while." She gestured to her leg.

"Do you plan to return once your leg is healed?"

"I don't know. I mean, yes, that would be nice, but I can't help but feel like things are shifting. Know what I mean?"

"I do. I'd felt this kind of heart nudge prior to Dave Cuttrey offering me the job in Canmore. Like there was something in the wind, but I didn't know what it was until he spoke to me."

Huh. It seemed like Jake was a man who was in tune with what God might be saying and doing these days.

"So, what do you think things might be shifting to?" he asked. "What would you like to do?"

"I don't know. All my life I've just wanted to dance. The past year I've wondered about dancing overseas like my friend Bailey has done. Or joining a dance group that performs around the country. I don't mind teaching, but I don't know if it's something I want to do for someone else for the rest of my days."

"Would you ever want to open your own studio?"

She snorted. "Do you know how much that would cost?"

"No."

She told him, and his eyebrows rose. "That's a lot."

"It's because you have to fit it out a certain way, with sprung floors and mirrors and all the equipment. Bailey has had her studio in Winnipeg for six years now, and it's only been how she's wanted it in the past year or so."

He nodded, his lips pressed together like he was thinking seriously about her words.

She poked his arm. "What are you thinking about?"

"I suppose you need to have the right kind of venue as well."

"Exactly. Parents aren't always keen to drop their kids off at a factory unit somewhere. It helps if the building the classes are in has a bit of class."

He nodded. "Would you want to open a dance studio in Calgary?"

"I don't think so. I'd know some people and have local connections, but even that is problematic. People in the dance world can be really competitive, and I'd hate to be regarded as stealing students from those dance schools I've worked with in the past."

"What about opening one somewhere else?"

"Like?"

"Lethbridge. Red Deer. Canmore." He studied her.

Her nose wrinkled. "To be honest, none of those places have ever really grabbed me."

He nodded, his lips twisting slightly in the corner, like he might be disappointed. Probably not though. Now he knew how messed up she was, he'd probably be happy to not have anything to do with her again.

"So, maybe opening a dance school or maybe not, huh?"

Run her own dance school? Since Bailey's question a few weeks ago, she'd thought about the possibility a few times. What she'd call it. What classes she'd offer. But she didn't dare think too long, because without funds it was little more than a pipe dream. And there wasn't any point in daring to dream those kinds of dreams if she'd never be able to walk properly again.

"To be honest, I'm just waiting to get the next doctor's

verdict. He made a comment the last time I saw him that things didn't seem to be progressing as they should."

"Aw, Poppy. I'm sorry."

"Nothing's for certain yet, but that's the thing. It's reminded me that nothing *is* for certain. All my life, I've just wanted to dance, and now there is a chance I might not be able to dance at all."

Compassion shone in his eyes. She had to duck her head. Blink hard against the tears.

"Please don't say you're sorry," she muttered. "I might cry if you do."

"Can I say that I am praying for you?"

Her throat clogged, forcing her to nod. "Th-thank you."

"Hey, you don't know what the doctors will say, so there's no point catastrophizing and imagining the worst. God is a God who heals, right? Jehovah Rapha, the Lord who heals."

"Yes." Her lips twisted. "Have you been taking a Bible course or something?"

He shook his head. "Just learned a few things from the school of life."

Hadn't they all? What to do, what not to do.

"Regardless of what happens," he continued, "God is still in control of your life, right?"

"Right." God was. And while it was easy to say, in moments like now when she felt like she was standing at a crossroads in life, she was especially glad that God was with her. That she could trust Him. Jake was so good to remind her of this. "I needed to hear this. Thank you."

"So even if you're not dancing overseas, or running your own dance studio, then God still has good plans for your life."

"Yes."

Yes. God *did* have good plans for her. She might not dance or live up to the dreams she'd once had, but she'd come to recognize God's goodness to her in recent months. God had been faithful. God still was faithful. And though she might need to pivot to something different to what she'd once imagined, it didn't change the fact that God still loved her, and had promised to be with her every step of the way.

She met Jake's smile, and new warmth stirred in her heart. The man was so good to remind her of God's promises.

His smile fed hope, then spilled truth. "I don't really know about a dance studio anyway. It's been interesting watching what happened with Bailey because of her name being attached to *Dance Off Canada*, and then with Luc Blanchard. I feel like if I was to open a studio it would be something similar, that I'd be known not for who *I* am, but who I'm related to. And I don't want people attending because of my brother's name or the fact that my sister-in-law is a TV reporter or my new brother-in-law is a famous actor."

"You don't need to tell me what it's like to live in the shadow of a more famous sibling."

See? Another thing they had in common. "That's two things."

"Two things?"

"Two things we have in common. We're both Christians, and we both have more famous brothers."

"I can think of a few more."

"Yeah?"

He tapped his thumb. "We're both proud Albertans."

"True."

Tapped his forefinger. "We both love our families."

"Yep."

"We both enjoy fishing."

"Whoa, hold it right there. That's a solid no from me."

"Hey, I didn't necessarily mean fishing for fish.'

Her eyes widened. "Are you saying I enjoy fishing for compliments?"

"I'm teasing."

"Hmm. Well, I was going to say we both have a cool sense of

humor, but apparently I'm the only one who has a good sense of humor, and yours is a little more cruel than cool."

"Hey! I might resemble that comment."

Her lips lifted. The man was wittier than she remembered. "I think you need to be careful. You're starting to make me think you're fun."

"Oh, you think I'm fun, do you?"

His husky tone dropped into her nervous system, sending a shiver down her back.

Her gaze fell to study his lips, then felt a pull of something that shifted her nearer him. Her lips parted, her eyelids fluttered then drifted closed, then...

"Hey, Poppy?"

Her eyes flew open.

His brow was creased. "I'm glad we're able to be friends."

"Friends, yes. Yes, of course." Embarrassment shimmered over her. What had he thought she was trying to do? "O-of course. Yes, you're right. Anything else would be foolish." Talk about foolish. What was she doing thinking she had a second chance? Had the wedding and moonlight drawn all sense from her brain?

"Hey, are you two coming in?" Jess called. "They're about to cut the cake, then do the last dance."

"Uh, sure." Poppy glanced at him, and he instantly rose and held out his hand.

"Come on. Let's get Pirate Peg back inside."

"Pirate Peg?"

"You've got a wooden leg, right?"

"You're so rude." She laughed, and pushed him, then almost overbalanced.

He caught her, drawing her close to his chest. "You need to be careful who you try to push around."

"Apparently."

He studied her, and she stared back.

"What is it?"

He shook his head. "Nothing."

That look wasn't nothing. But there was no easy way to ask him when he was holding out his arm and helping her return to the white tent. Inside, she joined her family, clapping as Cassie and Harrison cut the cake, using a ceremonial silver sword that had been found in one of the western town's buildings. Every so often Poppy would look for Jake, and he'd meet her eyes and smile, which made her heart smile too.

The last dance was called, and he asked her if she'd like to join him again, which she agreed to. She might've once hoped to impress some of these Hollywood types with her skills, but right now all she wanted was someone who was happy to take things slow, whose care for her was as obvious as the sparkle in the depths of his chocolatey eyes.

"You look happier," he murmured.

"I feel a lot lighter and more free," she admitted.

"Me too." He drew her closer still, and she had no option, but to rest her cheek against his chest.

And close her eyes, and wonder if maybe God was giving her a second chance after all.

CHAPTER 14

His mom's phone call came as he was eating his frozen dinner-for-one. He knew he'd have to answer her sooner or later. Might as well be now. "Hey Mom."

"So how did things go with Poppy?"

He smiled. There was never any beating around the bush as far as she was concerned. "Great." He shared about what had happened last weekend.

"Sounds like a real answer to prayer."

"God is so good."

"So, what now?"

"What do you mean?"

"I mean have you made arrangements for getting together again?"

"No." He'd danced that final dance with Poppy then she'd winced, and admitted she was tired. He'd immediately helped her to sit down, and when she'd been surrounded by friends and family who started looking at him with speculation in their eyes, he'd felt it was only prudent to escape.

He'd attended as Derek had asked. He'd spoken with Poppy

as God had wanted him to. And now it felt like things between them were good again, he didn't want to push for more. Well, he *did*, but wisdom whispered to hold back.

Especially as she'd made it fairly clear during their talk that she was happy to be friends. For a wild and crazy second he'd stupidly thought that maybe she wanted to kiss him, but he didn't want to stir up anything that was based on the physical, especially on a day that must've already been emotionally and physically draining. So he'd made that comment about being friends. She'd seemed okay with it, and he could've kicked himself at being so dumb to say it aloud. But friendship was better than flinging themselves into something that wasn't healthy. He wouldn't do that again.

"The factory is keeping me busy, Mom. But hey, you and Dad will have to come out for a visit. I've got plenty of room here."

"Now that sounds like a great idea. When would work for you?"

They discussed potential dates, his mom checking her scheduled shifts at the nursing home where she worked. Dad's work was less flexible, but he might be able to swing things to come visit too. Regardless, it'd be good to have his folks come visit and see his new home.

"Well, well, well. Jake Guillemette is back again."

He turned. Saw Martha Diamond again. "Martha. I didn't realize you attended church here."

She shrugged. "I don't normally, but my granddaughter is visiting me and wanted to come."

He glanced at the young woman hovering nearby. She didn't hold a candle to Poppy. But—he suppressed those feelings. They might have started anew, but they were only friends. He wouldn't assume or start imagining things. He'd been tortured enough by stubborn dreams, foolishly thinking she might've wanted to kiss him at the wedding. Daring to think more was only asking for trouble. Not when Poppy hadn't given any solid indication that she cared for him in that way. "Hi. I'm Jake."

"I'm Maggie." She was blonde too, but more a white-blonde, like she possessed Norwegian heritage.

He made small-talk for a while, itchy to leave. He didn't want to give Martha or Maggie any wrong ideas.

"Now, Jake, have you had any more thoughts about the studio?"

"It's still for sale?"

"Finding the right buyer is proving to be a challenge."

"You might need to lower the price a little."

"I might, for the right person."

He nodded. His phone buzzed in his back pocket. He drew it out. His mom. "Well, if you'll excuse me."

"Oh, before you go, I don't suppose you know of anything fun that young folk around here might like to do?"

He stared at Martha, a disconcerting niggle drawing suspicion. He glanced at Maggie. "Uh, there's plenty of nature trails and things."

She nodded, and he felt the sense to leave. "Excuse me. I really should take this. It's my mom."

"Oh, a woman loves a man who loves his mom, doesn't she?" Martha nudged Maggie.

He offered a twitch of a smile and backed away. "Nice to meet you."

"You too."

Okay, he was definitely getting out of here. Some might call him a hero, but he wasn't brave enough to take on Martha. She seemed like a woman on a mission, and knowing his mom would be here tomorrow, that seemed like too many headstrong women for any one man to deal with.

. . .

"Jakey, can you tell me what this is?"

He glanced at the kitchen, where his mom held aloft the pamphlet about the Diamond Dance Studio. "Oh, that's nothing."

"Are you taking *dance* lessons?"

"No."

"Hmm." She eyed him. "Not trying to impress a certain young lady who just so happens to be a dancer?"

"Nope."

"Then please explain?"

He sighed. He should've known his mom would ferret things out. Her offer to help him sort his space was really an invitation to search his house for clues on what he was really doing. It hadn't taken long.

"I was jogging past one day and saw it's up for sale. The owner gave that to me."

"Are you planning to buy a dance studio?"

"No. But I wondered…" He shrugged.

"You wondered if Poppy might be interested one day."

He shrugged again. "I haven't said anything to her."

"Why not?"

"I don't know. It felt like we're finally at a place where we're friends, and I didn't want to mess things up by suggesting she move here. That would just look shady."

"You don't know that."

No. But he didn't want to come across as pushy. "I don't want her to think I want her here."

"You don't want her here?"

"Okay, I do, but I don't want Poppy to think that."

"I have to admit, Son, that this is starting to confuse me. Do you still like her?"

"Yeah, but I'm trying to leave it to God. I don't want to wreck things."

"Yes, but I'm guessing Poppy would still like to know if you do have feelings for her. Women might be many things, but not many of us are mind readers."

"But you are, right?" he teased.

"Some of the time, yes."

He chuckled, and hugged her. "I'm glad you're here."

"And I'm glad to be here, to get a little glimpse of your life and what you're up to. But I would like to know why you haven't said anything to Poppy about it."

"Look, apart from it being awkward with Poppy, the lady who owns the studio is a little weird, a little intense. Then yesterday she randomly came to church and brought her granddaughter and basically told me I should take her out on a date."

Mom's eyebrows flew up. "And is this granddaughter someone you're interested in?"

"No."

"Because you still have feelings for Poppy," his mom stated.

He dipped his chin.

"And this elderly lady has never been to your church before?"

"I got the impression she's been trying out different churches trying to find me."

His mom winced. "That sounds a little stalker-ish."

He laughed. "That sounds a little dramatic, but yeah, maybe."

How bizarre. He wasn't the kind of guy other women chased. He was the kind they ignored, or quickly looked past. The equivalent to Maggie perhaps. Which sounded mean, but was probably just honest.

His mom eyed him with an intensity not too far from what Martha projected. "What?"

She shook her head. "Do you think Poppy wants to run her own studio?"

"When we talked she wasn't sure, so I don't know. I think a lot depends on what the doctor says."

"Hmm. When does she find out about that?"

"I don't know."

"Then maybe that's what a friend would do. Find out. Show they care." She tapped the pamphlet. "Just like a friend might tell a friend when a business opportunity came their way that they might be interested in."

"I asked about whether she'd want to run a studio but she said she's not sure."

"God can turn someone's heart to where He wants it to go. We saw that with Sylvie, didn't we?"

"Yeah." Who else but God could have softened the Goth girl's heart to such an extent?

"Our job is to trust God and to be faithful with what we've been given." She fingered the pamphlet again. "So talk to her, Jakey. Soon."

He nodded, but internally shrugged. That conversation felt a little too hard. Even for a man who others might consider brave.

His mom's challenge ate at him during the night. Kept him company as he worked during the next day. The next. He jogged past the studio—on the other side of the street—and noticed the little sign still perched there. Fine. He'd say something.

When he got home that night he found Poppy's phone number. Then wondered if it still was her number. His last message had been sent three years ago:

> I'm sorry.

He winced. Prayed. Then tapped out a new one, keeping things fairly innocuous in case this wasn't her number any more.

> Hey, hope you're doing well. I remembered it must almost be time for your next doctor's visit. How are things? Any news? Praying for you.

Then pressed send.

TEARS FLOODED her eyes as the doctor's report swirled around and around. Far from healing properly, her leg now needed to be broken again and the whole process started again. If she didn't, there was a chance she might never walk properly again.

How could she have thought God was working things out? This wasn't good. The prospect of months of more pain felt far too hard.

"I don't understand," she whispered, once she and Mom and Jess were back in the car. "I thought I'd be better by now."

"He said it was the years of training that has affected your bones."

That which had no doubt been exacerbated by the twist when she'd tried to help her dad. In other words, she had done this to herself. Again. It wasn't something she could blame anyone else for. "Why would God give me this desire to dance then take away the ability to dance again?"

"It's not forever," Mom reminded her. "Just for a season."

A season where she'd once again have to let Bailey know she couldn't support her. And now Bailey was pregnant, what was she going to do?

"It's better that the doctors deal with it properly once and for all than live with pain. I know it might seem like forever, but it's not. Just a few more months."

"It'll be winter by the time I can dance properly again." If she ever could.

But no. She didn't want to live defeated. She would get better. She had to.

As Jess drove to a city restaurant, she wiped her face, glanced at her phone. Realized she'd silenced notifications, so she turned them on.

Saw a message from Bailey. One from Cassie. Then one from Jake.

> Hey, hope you're doing well. I remembered it must almost be time for your next doctor's visit. How are things? Any news? Praying for you.

Her eyes pricked. The man who had messaged that today was a different man to the one who had messaged three years ago. She glanced back at their previous messages, her heart hitching at the flirty comments, the innuendo, the banter that had been surface only, nothing deep. Certainly nothing about prayer, nothing that demonstrated real caring. Not like he showed now.

"You okay?" Jess asked, eyeing her in the rear vision mirror.

"Yep."

"Anything I can do?"

Jess could get her a certain man to come give her a hug. But that man was far away, and he'd insisted on being friends, had backed away when she'd wanted more. So he probably wouldn't agree if she asked for a hug.

"I'll be okay," she muttered. She'd have to be.

"God's got you in the palm of His hand," Jess said. "I know this is hard but just wait. You'll see."

If anyone understood the challenges of waiting for God to bring healing, it was Jess. After last year's mental breakdown, she had taken months to get back to her happy self. But the Jess of today was different to the Jess before. She was nicer. Less busy. Less stressed. It hadn't been a pleasant season for her, but she had come through it.

They arrived at the restaurant and quickly ordered drinks. This was a pity meal, she knew, something to ease the challenging doctor's news.

Mom clasped her hand. "Poppy, I know today is hard, but it will get easier."

"I know." She glanced at Jess. "I was remembering before what you had to go through."

Jess nodded. "It wasn't easy, and it might sound strange but in some ways I'm now actually glad I went through that."

"Why?"

Jess sipped her water. "I thought I had to have it all together, that I had to juggle all the things. I didn't realize that I was already dropping the ball in lots of ways. I just couldn't see them."

"What balls were you dropping?" Poppy asked.

"Obviously my mental health. My relationships. I know I was a lot of hard work." She smiled wryly.

"Good thing we love you." Poppy smiled.

Mom nodded. "I feel for those who don't have loving families to support them in hard times."

"We've had more than our fair share of hard times in recent years," Poppy said.

"But we're still together. And we've always known that God is with us and gives us the strength we need." Mom turned to Poppy. "And that's the same for you too. Today is challenging, and you know that in upcoming weeks there will be more days of pain. But it's not forever. And if it is helping you to be strong then that's a good thing."

"That's right. What's that saying? Your comeback will be greater than your setback." Jess rolled her eyes. "Look at me with all the motivational cliches."

"It's almost like you're dating a sports guy," Poppy teased.

"Right?" Jess smirked.

Their waiter came, took their orders, then Mom and Jess went to the bathroom, giving Poppy space to think. What would her future look like? Another three months off dancing meant three months off to look at all her options. Where to live. What to do. Who to be. And just like Jess had acknowledged some of her shortcomings, so Poppy knew that in the past few years she hadn't been all she could be either. She'd leaned too hard into the Party Poppy persona and become someone she was not. Had let unforgiveness shape her into being bitter for too long, had drifted from God, even while playing the game and pretending she had not. She wanted to be different. To not chase fame. To not chase those things she knew wouldn't satisfy. She wanted God to fill those spaces. *God.* And not a relationship with someone who wanted her more than wanting God.

She blinked back tears. But no, this was important. Actually, this felt *immense*. But a good kind of immense. Like maybe God was giving her this opportunity to not just fill her life with more distractions but was actually drawing her heart back to Him. She propped her head in one hand. *Hey Lord, what is it You want from me? I want what You have for me. Your plans, not my own. Help me to see them, to walk in them, to* want *to walk in them.* For it was one thing to know *what* God wanted her to do. She'd proved this past year that it was quite another to *want* to do it.

"You're looking very serious there," Jess said, as she and Mom reseated themselves.

Oh, to be able to do something as simple as walk and sit down, without having to use crutches or rely on others. How could she have ever taken such things for granted?

"I think I'm going to have to reconsider my future," she admitted.

"Not dance?" Jess asked, her eyes wide.

She shook her head. "I can't even believe I'm thinking that.

But I don't think I can continue to help Bailey in the way I have. I don't want to live in Winnipeg. Not when it's so far away from home."

Mom nodded. "I know that you are worried about your father, but he will be okay. He's getting stronger every day." Hence why Mom had finally agreed to leave him at the ranch under Cassie's care, now Cassie had returned from her honeymoon. "You don't need to alter your plans because of him."

"I know. But I also don't feel like it's quite the same anymore. I used to feel jealous of you all and wanted to have fame too, but now I don't."

"Please." Jess rolled her eyes. "I'm not famous."

"You're super smart, though. And you have Tom, and he's pretty famous."

"He's about the most normal pro hockey guy out there."

"Apart from his terrible jokes. That's pretty abnormal if you ask me."

Jess's jaw dropped. "I can't believe you'd say that. He's funny."

"Exactly. Funny, but not necessarily in a ha ha way." Poppy smirked.

"Wow. I can't believe I was feeling sorry for you five minutes ago."

"Girls, not when we're out. Please behave."

Poppy caught Jess's smile and smothered a giggle as their waiter returned with their food.

"So what do you think you would like to do?" Mom asked when he had gone.

"I don't know." Jake had asked the same.

"Would you like to run your own studio?" Jess asked.

"Maybe. It's hard to know when I don't even know if this next surgery will work."

"You need to have faith that it will."

She nodded. Faith. Faith that God would heal her properly this time. And faith that whatever lay in her future, He would prepare her heart for it. A job. A career. And Jake.

She glanced at her phone. She should reply.

Lord, have Your way. Your will be done. Not mine.

CHAPTER 15

What could he do when the woman he cared for was going through surgery and he wanted to show he cared but not too much? It was the same dilemma he'd faced when she'd sent her message.

> Doctor said it hasn't healed properly. Need new surgery. This time with plates.

He hadn't known what to say except reply with an

> I'm sorry.

Plates for a dancer couldn't be good, right? Yet asking that via messenger felt too raw. Even if messaging her this way felt strangely safe. Like they could be personal, but not too personal. He wanted to give her distance, but still show he cared.

So what then? Send flowers? Was that too much? Saying he was praying for her felt like it was growing a little thin. Anyone could send thoughts and prayers. But sending something tangible put this tenuous friendship into something more like relationship territory. Which this wasn't, despite his mom's pleas for him to make an effort.

"I still don't feel any sense to chase her," he told her, the next time she called on the phone.

Mom had huffed. "Well, I'll just be praying that God directs her heart where it needs to go."

Mom had enjoyed her visit, and had gone home the day before Poppy had finally responded to his text.

And because he didn't want to stir up his mom's interest, he wasn't about to ask her now. So what would a friend send a friend after surgery? He didn't have the cash of Harrison to spoil her. He didn't have the wacky jokes of Jess's boyfriend, Tom. He'd met Tom at the wedding, and that man was beyond ready to be a dad with the dumbness of his jokes. But he made Jess laugh, so that was the main thing.

What did Jake have? Nothing romantic, which was probably just as well. He did have God. *Hey Lord, what do you want me to say to encourage her?*

He went for a run, prayed the whole time, then finally felt a verse stir.

> Hey, I've been praying for you with your surgery today. Here is a verse I hope encourages you like it does me. 2 Corinthians 4.17-18 'This light and momentary trial is preparing for us an eternal weight of glory beyond all comparison, as we look not to the things that are seen.' It might not seem very light right now, but it's not forever. Especially if we keep focused on God.

In case she'd thought that too heavy, he'd sent another one.

> And look, here's a picture of a pretty tree.

He'd snapped a pic of a dogwood that was changing color as cooler temperatures hit and sent it.

Three Creek Ranch might be only an hour away, but winter hit sooner here. Already the summer plague of tourists had mostly left, leaving the local stalwarts. There'd be leaf peepers soon, one of the long term locals had assured, then those wanting winter sports soon. But for now in this brief dip of population he was enjoying discovering more of what his new home offered.

Like the dance studio which still hadn't sold.

Should he send Poppy information about it? It felt presumptuous, and he honestly didn't know if he'd cope too well if she dismissed it out of hand. But then, maybe his mom was right. God could direct Poppy's heart where it needed to go. And Jake would have to trust God that if it was meant to be steered toward him that that would happen. And that if it was meant to be directed another way, then that would happen too.

His phone lit with a message. His heart lit when he saw who it was from.

> Thank you. In pain right now but praising God for pain meds and for friends who care.

Friends. His heart fell. See? That was all.

THE NEXT WEEK he sent another message.

> Hey, it's been a week. How are you doing?

> Look who's keeping count! Getting better, in Jesus's name.

He smiled, glad for the chance to smile after a tough week of Dave coming down hard on every little mistake. "I don't pay you to let mistakes slide, Jake."

"It won't happen again," he'd assured. *In Jesus's name*, he'd silently added.

He sent Poppy another verse he'd found helpful this week. Romans 8:31 "If God is for us, then who can be against us?" then a picture of a squirrel in his back yard.

She sent back a smiley face. And a question:

> Is that your yard?

> Yes.

THE WEEK after he sent another message.

> Hey, been thinking of you. How is your dad doing?

Dad is fine, her message came almost straight away.

> Here's his number if you want to call. I'm fine too, in case you wanted to know.

Okay, so that had gone well. He messaged back:

> I'm glad.

Then sent a picture of Canmore's main street. Her message came back fast.

> What's with all these pictures you keep sending?

Oh. His heart dipped.

> I thought you might like seeing them, seeing you can't get out much right now.

> I'm sorry. My leg is really sore today. I do appreciate the thought. Maybe one day when I'm better I can come see you there.

Yes. His fist-pumped.

> That'd be good.

> Let's make a date, then.

His heart skipped several beats. But no. She wasn't talking about a date kind of date with him. Just a plan to get together when she was well.

THEIR MESSAGING SOON INCREASED, from weekly to twice weekly, to more. Jake kept sending pictures, offering glimpses of his new town, hoping they'd stir her interest and seed more thoughts about visiting him one day. It helped that Canmore was insanely pretty in Fall, that the mountain vistas were glorious, inspiring from every angle. And the fact he could be inspired pretty much every time he walked outside led to a lot of lifted spirits, even as the temperature plummeted as winter drew near.

On his last jog past the Diamond Dance Studio the sign still remained. He smiled. Maybe God was keeping it for Poppy, for when she finally could come visit. He'd been half tempted to go visit her, to bring her here himself, but that felt a little too much like pressure, and he didn't want to do that. Not when she needed to feel like she could own such a decision for herself.

So he kept working, kept praying, kept trusting, kept reading the Bible, kept attending church. And as they kept messaging, he felt like they were slowly, finally, becoming friends.

THANKSGIVING WAS when her family gathered and remembered all the good things that had happened over the past year. And this year, with Cassie married, Hannah pregnant, and Dad still alive, felt like a most wonderful year, even despite the challenges Poppy had faced herself.

At least this second round of surgery had been a lot easier than the first. It probably helped to have gone through this experience and to know what to expect. Patience wasn't one of her strong suits, but she'd developed a lot more of it lately, her jigsaw puzzle building now en pointe.

It had definitely helped to get Jake's messages regularly. She understood her friends had their own lives to live and couldn't keep constantly checking in on her, but to have his weekly messages, now almost daily, gave brightness to those days when he did. Sometimes it was a verse, sometimes it was a photo, sometimes simply encouraging words. He obviously had a deep faith, deeper than hers, anyway, but these months of missing church had forced her to delve into the Bible too. She watched online church but it wasn't the same.

She'd asked him about his church, and he'd sent a picture of a school hall. She'd thought he'd mistaken what she meant then realized he was showing her the kind of church he attended. No spire or pews, but that was okay. He'd sent another picture from inside, obviously when the congregation were worshipping, judging from the raised hands and words on a big screen. She'd like to see that place one day.

In fact, she'd like to revisit Canmore soon. She didn't remember it being quite so quaint and cute. He'd posted pictures of a farmer's market, a library, meals from various restaurants he'd dined at, all of which looked so good.

She studied the mountain of food on the table before her. Mom had asked people to contribute today, and Poppy had made a fruit salad. Not especially imaginative, but she could chop fruit and stay out of the way of those in the kitchen.

Cassie and Harrison had brought a baked turkey from their newly renovated cottage on the ranch. Franklin and Hannah had brought several pies—store bought—along with Hannah's mom. And Jess and Tom had brought salads, along with big smiles. Seeing all the couples brought a reminder that she was alone. It was enough to make her wonder if she should've asked Jake, but he'd indicated he was visiting his own family in Red Deer, so she let that wish slide. It was enough to be thankful that they were friends, even if sometimes she wanted more.

Like when she went to sleep and imagined his lips on hers. His hands on—No. She had to take those thoughts captive and ask God to renew her mind.

She glanced across at her father. He was eating a little slower these days. "How are you feeling, Dad?"

"Glad to be here with you all."

Mom nodded, looking teary as she always did whenever he said something similar. "We should never take time together for granted."

"Exactly." Cassie looked across at Poppy. "How are you feeling?"

Poppy didn't see Cassie quite so much these days, seeing as she was living with Harrison in their cottage. It felt strange to live in the farmhouse without her. Cassie had been a fixture here all her life. "I'm okay."

"You seem happier." Harrison's smile reduced the sting of his comment. How unhappy had she appeared?

"I'm more content."

"Is Jake not coming?" Hannah asked.

"Why would he?"

"Who's Jake?" Hannah's mom asked.

"He's Poppy's *friend*," Jess smirked.

"Your boyfriend?"

"No. Just a friend." At the looks her siblings gave her, her cheeks heated. "What?"

"Hands raised who thinks Jake would like to be more than just Poppy's friend," Cassie teased.

Everyone raised their hands, Mom and Dad included. Apart from Hannah's mom, who looked at her bemused.

"Well, he's not. So there."

"He could be, if you wanted him to be," Cassie said.

"He's made it pretty clear he wants to be my friend, nothing more."

"Nothing more? Is this the same man who is messaging you nearly every day?" Jess asked.

"Yeah, I don't message my friends as often as that," Franklin said.

"Nope, he doesn't," Tom said.

Poppy raised her eyebrows. "Who says you're his friend?"

"Rude."

She smiled, glad the man could cope with her tease. He had to cope if he was going to fit in. It made her wonder whether Jake would ever feel comfortable with her family. Well, he certainly was in some ways, but in others, he probably could afford to spend more time with them.

"He's also the man who keeps sending her pictures of where he lives," Jess said.

"Do you mind?" Poppy mock-glared at her. "Haven't you got anything more interesting to say?"

"Actually…" Tom glanced at Jess, who seemed to glow.

Uh oh. Only one guess what this could be.

She eyed Jess's left hand. This looked like a repeat of what had happened last Christmas. Was this to be repeated each year at a family holiday? If that was the case, would that mean next year was her turn? She shivered.

"I thought you all might like to know that I have something very special to be thankful for," Tom said.

"What's that?" Cassie asked, her smile saying she guessed too.

"I asked Jess to marry me and—"

"I said yes!" Jess beamed.

"Congratulations!" They were swamped with hugs and congratulations, and demands to see the ring.

Jess laughed. "We don't have one yet."

"I figured I'd rather get one that she wants, that's good for her work with animals so she doesn't need to ever take it off," Tom admitted.

"I suspect he just thinks I'm fussy." Jess laughed again.

Yeah, no. Her sister might've once been a stress head, but she was far more low maintenance than people credited her, not caring about her clothes or appearance. Not like Poppy had.

She eyed her fingernails. The Poppy of before was long overdue for a manicure, but these days she didn't care. She rarely was out in company, so her appearance didn't matter. Of course, if someone who was *not her boyfriend* should suddenly drop by then she might get in a tizzy and regret it. But as he was far away then she didn't need to fuss. Which was nice to not worry about stuff like that. It proved appearances really didn't matter. It was nice to actually be able to focus on what really was important. Like the fact that he loved God. The fact that he was kind. Thoughtful.

"So, when do you think you'll get married?"

Tom slid a look at Jess who nodded. "We actually wondered about Christmas—"

"Christmas? That's two months away!"

"—then we realized that's probably too much considering everything else that happened this year, so we're hoping for June. As soon as possible, anyway."

Mom fanned herself. "When you first spoke to Derek and I

about wanting to get married, I had assumed it would be next year."

"Sorry, Mom." Jess leaned across and kissed her cheek. "I don't want to cause any panic attacks or other ones."

"Thank you. Much appreciated."

The hum of happy conversation buzzed around the table, until Franklin caressed his wife's baby bump. "It's probably a good thing you won't be getting married then. Not when we'll have enough excitement around Christmas."

"How are you feeling, Hannah?" Mom asked. The question of the day, apparently.

"I'm good, but getting tired. I'll be taking leave at the end of the month, at least from in front of camera, so that will be nice."

Poppy knew Hannah had experienced a huge level of comments about her looks; it was hard to imagine what comments she'd been facing now she was pregnant.

Franklin glanced at Poppy. "And then there was one." He raised his eyebrows.

She raised hers, but didn't bite.

He smiled. "Do you want me to message him, get him to call in on his way back?"

Yes. No prizes for guessing who he referred to. "No."

"You sure?"

"Of course she'd like him to come see her," Cassie said. "What's it been? Eight weeks since the wedding?"

"Nearly nine," she mumbled. She'd counted the other day.

"Nearly nine weeks without seeing the man." Cassie turned to Harrison. "Imagine that!"

"Don't have to imagine," he said, kissing her hand. "Don't want to do that again."

"But at least they have been messaging regularly," Jess said, smirking at Poppy.

"Could we please change the topic?"

"But this is so fun. What was the last picture he sent you?"

Her heart thumped. Yesterday, he'd sent a picture of a dance studio, one with a sign in the window saying For Sale, Enquire Within. She'd wondered if Jake had meant something.

"Oh, was it that private?"

"No."

"Prove it," Jess said.

"Fine." She got out her phone, showed her sister, who soon passed her phone around. "See?"

"He sent you a photo of a dance studio for sale?" Hannah asked. "Are you wanting to open your own place?"

"I don't know," she admitted. "It could be a good opportunity, but I haven't investigated. Things like that would cost so much to open that I'd never have the cash, even if I wanted to anyway."

Harrison smiled at her. "I happen to know some people sitting here who might be able to loan you some."

"Thanks, but I'll need to think about it." Because it was one thing to potentially accept money from her brother, another from her in-laws.

"So, Jake the Great wants you to buy a dance studio in the town where he now lives. I wonder why?" Cassie smirked.

"You'll have to ask him that," she grouched.

"Maybe I just will." Cassie grabbed Poppy's phone.

"What are you doing?"

Cassie kept typing away. "Just letting someone know that he should stop by on his way back to Canmore."

"Cassie, no!" She snatched her phone back, and went to delete the message. Then saw it had been delivered.

Her sisters laughed, drawing the others' smiles.

"That's enough, girls," Mom said in her warning voice. "Now, are we ready for dessert?"

"I'm always ready for dessert," Tom murmured, sliding a look at Jess that caused her to blush, and drew a curl in Poppy's stomach.

Maybe these two should get married sooner rather than later. She knew what happened when desire got the better of good intentions. She ducked her head.

And maybe, just maybe, she should see if there was a way to see Jake. And see if the feelings stirred by thoughts of him could be fanned into something warmer than friendship.

CHAPTER 16

*J*ake got back from Red Deer, then immediately checked the message from Poppy. Then immediately wanted to kick himself for not checking it earlier. She wanted him to visit? He could have. So easily. He'd driven straight past the turn off to the ranch, but hadn't dared. There hadn't been any great sense of urgency, not like that time before when obviously God had wanted him to go help Derek. So maybe God didn't want him connecting with Poppy like that. Not yet, anyway. It felt enough that he'd finally sent her a picture of Diamond Dance Studio, which had not yet received any reply from her. Well, hadn't. Until today.

He'd wondered what she thought he'd meant by him sending that picture. He knew what he meant. But it still felt too soon to say it out loud or even via text. So he did his best to give it to God, and let Him have his way.

He could still message her though.

> Sorry I didn't get your message in time.

Her reply came quickly:

> Hope you had a good day.

He sent a picture of his family's roast dinner. She sent one back of her family's lunch. He sent an emoji of smiling stuffed cheeks. She sent a gif of someone collapsing on a couch. Then she sent another message.

> Please excuse that message from before. My phone got hijacked.

Oh. Disappointment crowded his chest. She didn't want him to visit?

> Okay.

> Wait.

Her response came so fast he wondered if she'd been composing it before he'd replied.

> I just realized how that sounded. Sorry. Of course it would be nice to see you. But I'm guessing you're now at home, right?

> Yes.

She sent an awkward smile emoji.

He didn't know what to send back. In some ways he was getting tired of this messaging without saying the things he really wanted. In other ways, he knew that as soon as he said those things he really wanted to say, he was opening a can of worms that couldn't easily be closed.

He'd tried to intrigue her, tried to pique her interest, but keeping her at a distance was getting harder. Especially now he'd had a taste of anticipation. Now he knew the sharp pain of disappointment. "God, I wish You'd give me a sign if she cares."

He put away the leftovers in the fridge, toed off his shoes, cranked up the heat. Glanced at his phone again. The screen lit with an unread message.

> Are you still there?

> Yes.

That was safe. And true.

When her next message didn't soon come, he went and showered. He was obviously as much a glutton for punishment as he ever was. But seeing Ryan and Sylvie and their little baby today had only reinforced how much he wanted a family of his own. Especially over here, where he felt a little lonely. Maybe he should get a dog.

Mom had not had any sympathy for him, telling him straight that he needed to ask the woman out for goodness' sake. Well, that was easier said than done. And while he'd tried to explain that they'd made a tentative arrangement to meet together, she'd shaken her head saying he could do better than that. And yeah, maybe he could. But probably not while she still had a broken leg and limited mobility.

He toweled off, threw a load of laundry in the washing machine, then padded down the stairs to where his phone was charging. He'd check one more time then go to bed. He had an early start tomorrow. "Hey, God, please help me to cope with her rejection."

He looked at his phone, his heart flickering.

> I wish I could see you.

His heart thudded. Maybe this was the time to get real. He slowly typed out

> Ditto.

She sent a heart.

His own heart skidded. What did she mean by that? He sent a

> ?

Then his phone rang. It was her. He moved to answer then saw she was wanting a video call. So he answered, heart swelling at the sight of her. "Hi."

"Hi yourself." Her eyebrows rose. "And hello."

"Oh." He lifted the camera so it only saw his face. "I forgot I wasn't wearing a shirt. I just had a shower, and…" That was probably TMI, judging from the way she bit her lip.

Then she smiled. "I was only thinking that it would be easier to talk than to message. My fingers were getting sore."

"You don't use voice to text?" he teased.

"No."

"Neither do I."

She laughed. Then sobered. "I meant it before. I'm sorry about that message my sister sent. Then I'm sorry I made it awkward again. Because I would like to see you."

"And I'd like to see you."

Her smile grabbed him around the lungs and gently squeezed.

He could say something about how pretty she looked, how her smile was beautiful, her eyes… but he didn't want this—whatever *this* was—to be focused on stuff like that. He wanted real. Wanted depth. Not what whatever they'd shared before had been based on. "I've enjoyed our conversations."

"Me too." Her smile turned shy. "It's been really nice getting to know you this way."

"I agree."

"Even if I still don't know exactly why you sent that image of the dance studio."

Here went nothing, then. "I just thought it was interesting to see a studio for sale not too far from where you live, especially when I've been praying for you, and you've been praying about the future."

"So… there wasn't anything significant about you sending me that?"

"You mean the fact that it is here?"

She nodded.

"Are you asking if I want you to live nearby?"

She nodded again.

His throat dried. He could answer this with the simple truth, or he could skirt around the edges and not lie but not scare her off with the bald truth either. The truth? Yes, he wanted her nearby. But the alternative was equally correct. "I just thought it might be good for you to see what some of your options might be."

"Oh."

Should he have admitted the truth? "It would be good to have you nearby too," he added.

Her head tilted, as if unsure.

Clearly he'd mucked that up. Must be time to change the subject. "How is your leg?"

"The last test seems to show that things are healing better this time."

"That's great! When does your cast come off?"

"They're putting me in a brace this Friday."

"So soon?"

"It sure doesn't feel too soon to me."

"I bet." He swallowed. Prayed for favor. "Does this mean you might be able to come visit me soon?"

"Are you sure you can't come visit me?" she asked.

He drew in a breath, studied her face. A face he still dreamed of, still longed to kiss again. "I wish I could. But Dave has us working long hours until Christmas. We're entering the initial start-up phase and there are lots of things to stay on top of in order to keep going strong."

"Even on weekends?" she asked, clearly disappointed.

"On Saturdays, yes. Sundays we have off, but I have meetings scheduled with Dave in the afternoons."

"So if I was to come, I could see you during church then come home?"

"If you came, I'd find a way to make it work."

She nodded. "Then... is it possible for me to come see you next weekend? Mom said she's free to bring me, and it'd be good to do it before too long. Especially when we don't know how long the dance studio will still be for sale."

"What about your leg?"

"Oh, that's only if the doctor is okay, of course."

He nodded. "So you want to come next Sunday? I'm not sure if the owner will be open then."

"Is... is it possible to get her number? I could call her and then let you know and we could see if she's available and if that works for you."

"Okay. I'm pretty sure I have her number here somewhere. Hold on a moment."

He opened a drawer, found that pamphlet from long ago, and reeled off the number.

"Thanks."

"It'll be good to see you," he said.

"It'll be good to see you." She smiled.

And he carried that smile to bed with him, and when he woke it was to see another text from her.

> Can next Saturday work at all?

Saturday? He'd make it work somehow.

> Yes.

"How are you feeling about this?" Mom slid a glance in Poppy's direction.

"I don't know why but I feel nervous." She slid damp palms down her jeans, her gaze returning to outside. "But Canmore sure is prettier than I remember."

"Mm. Some people call Banff the prettiest town in these parts but I've always preferred Canmore. It feels more like a town where people live rather than overly touristy."

"And they pretty much share a similar view." An iconic main street with mountains soaring beyond.

The town was dressed in festive colors, with pumpkins adorning windows and Fall-colored wreaths everywhere. "It's really pretty."

"Did you want to drive past where the studio is first then go to the factory?"

Poppy glanced at the time. "I think we should go to the factory first. Even though I'm aching to see the studio I don't want to take up too much of Jake's time, not when I know he's so busy."

"Good plan."

And yes, while she longed to see the studio, she had another yearning too. One that would be satisfied as soon as she met Jake. It had been far too long since she'd seen him properly. That video call didn't count. Even if she couldn't forget the sight of his bare chest.

Mom turned into a different street, one that led to an industrial area, and drove to the factory site where Cuttrey Engineering was an obvious newly-built addition. She admired the new building and the freshly planted landscaping. It certainly looked very professional.

She texted him:

> We're here! Just out the front.

> I can see you.

She glanced up. Saw him standing, thick jacket on, arms crossed, smiling as Mom parked. And oh, the desire to leap from the car and run to him, put her arms around him, feel him close. But no. The doctor yesterday had said she needed to take tremendous care with her leg, that it was still healing, and if she didn't want problems down the track she needed to invest the time to let it heal properly now. So she unclipped her seat belt, then opened the door, then jumped as she realized he was standing there. "Uh, hi."

"Hi Poppy." His dark eyes lit as he smiled, then he ducked his head. "Hi Leonie. Thank you for going out of your way to do this."

"Oh, I'm overdue a little escape from the ranch, so thank you for providing the opportunity to do so."

He grinned. "Any time."

Poppy's heart shivered. He sounded like he really wanted her to visit again. Like he wanted Poppy here again.

He ducked down. "So, tell me how I can help. Do you need help getting out of the car?"

"Um, if you can please pass me my crutch, then I can swing my leg out if you keep the door opened wide."

"Sure." He did so, and helped her stand. "Hi."

"Hello." His nearness tickled her senses. "Um, can I...?"

"Can I give you a hug?" he asked softly.

Yes. She nodded, more stupid tears springing to life at his understanding. She never used to be this weak, but something about this man had always managed to sneak past the closed drawbridge of her heart. Like he understood her. They were on a similar wavelength.

He wrapped his arms around her, and she closed her eyes and let him hold her, drinking in his strength, his scent, his care. And that was the difference. This wasn't just based on physical awareness but awareness of his thoughtfulness, that he respected her, that he hadn't pushed. It was almost like he was waiting for her to make the first move, like he wouldn't impose again. And his sensitivity toward her made this all the more special.

"I missed you," she whispered.

"I missed you more," he murmured into her hair. Then he released her, helping her balance as she wobbled. Then gave her mom a quick hug too. "Hi Leonie."

"Hello Jake. You look taller than the last time I saw you."

He shrugged. "Might be my boots. It's pretty cold inside."

"Frosty the Snowman-type cold, or just normal cold?" Poppy teased.

"We're not quite at Frosty temperatures yet."

She chuckled, and he smiled, and her heart glowed.

He took them on a tour, but she didn't care too much about the factory per se. It was more interesting to see how his face shone with enthusiasm for his work, the fact he took obvious pride in what he'd done, even though he constantly referenced Dave Cuttrey as his mentor, humbly acknowledging that he owed everything to the man. "And God."

"Amen," Mom said, which Poppy echoed slowly.

The man was humble. Once upon a time she had wanted a man who would make his mark upon the world. Someone rich, someone famous, someone like the men her sisters were involved with. Now she realized she wanted to be better because this man made her softer, made her realize that all the riches and fame in the world couldn't compare with the peace that was found by knowing Jesus. That yes, they had messed up together, but perhaps God had used that to break them and reshape them for His purposes. To know Him more. To get to know—really know—each other more.

He finished the tour, then said apologetically, "I probably went on too long, eh?"

"No," Poppy rushed to assure him. "I think what you've done is amazing."

His smile was wry as he shrugged. "I think it's remarkable what can be accomplished in a relatively short amount of time."

He might be talking about the factory, but his words held true for them too. God had changed Jake, had changed Poppy, too. What did that mean for them? For their relationship? *Was this even a relationship?*

"I know you have a meeting with Martha at the studio soon, but I thought maybe afterwards we could have lunch together. If you like."

"That'd be great!" Poppy said. "Where do you suggest?"

He told her about a deli café near the studio and asked her to call when she was done and he'd meet them there.

"Sounds great. See you then." She smiled.

His smile softened. "I imagine the studio isn't perfect, but I hope you can see the potential. If not this one, then maybe another somewhere else sometime."

But now she'd visited, and realized how cute the town was, she didn't want a different one. She wanted to be near him. Oh, how she hoped this one would work. *Lord, please let this work. But Your will, not mine.*

"It'll be interesting to see it," Mom said. "Come on Poppy. We better get you back so you're not late."

He helped Poppy back in the vehicle, and gently squeezed her hand. "I wish I could come with you, but I sense it's better you do this on your own. Just mention you're my friend."

She nodded. "I'll see you after."

"See you soon." He smiled. "Thanks again, Leonie."

"I live to serve," Mom said dryly.

Poppy laughed and waved goodbye.

"I like to hear that," Mom said as she steered back into the main part of town.

"What?"

"You, laughing. You do that more when he's around."

Oh. "I hadn't realized."

"Something I've wanted for all my girls is for them to find a Christian partner who can help them relax. It's tricky when you're all so focused and high achievers in your own different ways."

"I haven't felt like I've achieved anything much in recent times."

"You underestimate yourself. These past few months have certainly been trying, there's no denying that. But you've also grown up so much. It's like the real Poppy has emerged, a kinder, more patient Poppy to the one we knew before."

"You make it sound like I was mean."

"Not mean, just… a little abrasive at times. A little self-focused, perhaps."

Oh. "Ouch."

"Which we all can be, especially when we're young, and we've had success and a taste of independence at an early age. I think life mellows us, and experiences like what you've gone through can really be the making of a person. It's only when we go through fire that the dross can be burned away."

Old Poppy would've just gotten offended at her mom's remarks. New Poppy knew there was truth there. "I've been so immature, haven't I? I'm sorry for being so drossy."

"You don't need to apologize. It's called growing up." Mom chuckled.

"What?"

"You like him, don't you?"

"Is it that obvious?"

"Telling a man you think he's amazing implies that, yes."

Her cheeks heated. "Well, he has done really well. He's nothing like the man I used to know." Oh. She bit her lip. Awkward. She didn't want to remind her mom that she and Jake shared a past. That wasn't embarrassing at all.

"I suspect that just as you've changed over the years, so he has too. Which is good. Especially as he seems to be walking closely with God now. And you're walking more closely too. A mother can't be sorry about that."

"So… you like him then?" Her heart hovered, waiting for her mom to respond, as she steered back into the street where the studio was located.

"I will always like the man who saved my husband's life. And if he proves to be a man who my daughter loves, then I will love him too."

More foolish emotion forced her to blink hard.

"Now, are you ready to see the dance studio?"

No. She felt like one sharp look might puncture her self-control and all the emotion within might leak. But God was with her. "Lord, give me wisdom."

"Amen."

Poppy raised her head. "Let's do this."

CHAPTER 17

The dance studio was everything warm and welcoming. Martha Diamond, on the other hand, was not. She eyed Poppy with a disconcerting stare. "So, you're Jake's friend."

"Yes." The little woman had the lithe frame of a former dancer, but her face was all angular and sharp, living up to her name.

"And how do you know each other?"

Why was that any of her business? Poppy was about to answer when her mom spoke, "Oh, her brother has been friends with Jake's brother for years."

"I see." Her features relaxed.

Poppy glanced at her mom. Why had she said it like that?

"And you've hurt yourself, I see." Martha's voice drew her attention back to her.

"I was dancing in Winnipeg when I landed badly and broke my tibia. Then discovered a few weeks ago that it wasn't healing properly so I had to have surgery and start the process again."

The hard glint in Martha's eyes faded. "It's been a challenging few months then. I understand. My husband died last year, which is why I decided I couldn't continue the studio anymore."

"I'm so sorry. That must be so difficult for you."

Martha nodded. "Especially when he was the one who built this place. See the floors? Well, perhaps you shouldn't jump on them. But they're fully sprung. Herbie did all that work himself. He put up all the mirrors. Arranged the windows so it's beautiful and light here."

"It's a lovely space. It feels quite airy."

"That's what I wanted it to feel like. It gets cold up here, but I always wanted people to feel like they could come and feel like this was a warm and inviting place to dance."

"Have you danced professionally?"

Martha nodded. "I did stints in Toronto and Montreal. I once did an off-Broadway show."

As Martha reminisced, Poppy realized that was an avenue in. She needed to find a way to connect. "My friend Bailey Donovan—Bailey Blanchard now—has danced on *Dance Off Canada*. Have you ever seen that show?"

"Never watched it." She sniffed. "The types of movement they call dancing on that kind of show is abominable to my way of thinking."

"Oh." Well, that had been a fail of an idea. Although how someone could judge when she claimed to not have watched the show seemed weird. "I know Bailey has enjoyed the chance to show that dancing can be accessible to all kinds of people. It's something that I've enjoyed doing at our studio in Winnipeg."

"So you've run a studio before?"

"Well, Bailey was the main person, but yes, I helped. I've been teaching for nearly six years now."

"Hmm. You must've started very young."

She nodded. "There's something so wonderful about taking a beginner who lacks confidence and giving them the tools they need to be successful."

"Yes. I agree. So why Canmore? Why not continue where you were?"

She sensed it wasn't a good idea to say anything about Jake. So she offered the alternative truth. "My dad had a heart attack a few months ago and I realized I didn't want to be too far away. My family lives just outside Calgary, so Canmore is a good distance from home."

"How far?"

"About an hour away."

"That's too far to commute in cold weather. Have you got somewhere to stay?"

"Uh, no." She shot her mom a look. Martha was right. That trip would be hard in winter. She really needed to live closer, but she'd seen how much apartments around here could cost. Way out of her price range. What would she do?

Martha's eyes narrowed. "You wouldn't be staying with Jake, would you?"

Her cheeks flushed. "Of course not."

Martha eyed her. Nodded. "I don't approve of young women sharing houses with young men. Unless they're married, of course."

Poppy pressed her lips together. Far from being a simple viewing of the dance space, this woman seemed intent on interrogation. And rather too interested in her connection to Jake.

"There is a small room behind the office that has been used as a little bedsit when the weather has been particularly terrible. Come."

Poppy followed to the room. It didn't have a bed, but one could easily fit in. And with the bathroom facilities and tiny kitchenette off the office, it was actually a better set up than Bailey's studio. "You've thought of everything."

"I wanted it to be the perfect studio. Which is why I've said no to the many other interested parties that have wanted this space. They wouldn't care about the sprung floors or the history of the place. They'd rip it out and put in another generic store like you see everywhere."

"I wouldn't do that."

"No. I can see you appreciate this studio."

So maybe there was some hope after all. Poppy glanced at her mom who nodded. "So, Martha, what kind of price are you talking?" Her heart hammered. Until she knew the price she wouldn't know if this was viable or not. She had some savings, but would likely have to borrow from the bank of Mom and Dad. Or Franklin.

Martha named her price, and Poppy's heart fell. There was no way she'd ever be able to afford that. Asking her family for that kind of money was impossible. "I, uh, will need to think about it. And get back to you."

"Hmph. I thought you would've snapped it up, but maybe you're not as keen as you made yourself out to be."

"I am keen. It's just... it's more than I thought it would be," she admitted.

"Well, it is freehold, and close to town. With excellent parking nearby." Martha coughed. "Just don't take too long. I've had plenty of interest."

Had she? She'd gotten the impression from the dusty For Sale sign that perhaps it wasn't as popular as Martha believed. Still, the fact remained that she couldn't afford it. Not right now.

"Well, thank you for your time. Would you mind if I took a video of the space? I'd like to show my potential investors." Such a fancy term for her family and Bailey, whom she knew would be interested, too.

"I suppose so," Martha agreed grumpily.

The woman really didn't seem to care about selling her property, Poppy thought as she filmed the video. Maybe she didn't have a dance school anymore because she'd frightened all the students away.

"Can I ask when you closed the dance school?"

"When my husband got sick. So it's been closed for nearly two years now."

"And where have all the students gone? Is there another school nearby?"

"There is one other. But it's not as good as mine."

Her heart sank a little further. Far from being the exclusive option for the locals, it seemed she would have competition, and be forced to build up her own clientele and pay far beyond what she could afford. Right now this didn't feel like a God idea. This felt like a bust.

"Okay, well, thank you for your time. I've really appreciated seeing this space. It is lovely."

"You don't sound like you'll be back," Martha said, way too observantly.

"I'll need to talk to the bank about whether I can afford it. Because it is more than I expected, especially considering I'd need to build my client list from scratch."

"Oh, I could give you their numbers. We could add that in for free."

"Really?"

"Obviously I won't be using them."

"But if they are two years out of date, then you may find it's not worth it," Mom said softly.

Martha's eyes narrowed, and Poppy figured it was time to make their escape. "Well, thanks again for your time. It's been most illuminating."

"Don't forget to make an offer soon. Otherwise it'll be too late."

Panic rose, the fear of missing out, and she nodded, clutched the ancient brochure Martha thrust at her, and blindly exited. Then nearly slipped on the footpath.

Mom steadied her, just as Jake had done before. "Well?"

She sucked in a deep breath of fresh air. Exhaled the disappointment. "I don't think I want to talk here. Who knows if she's still listening?"

Mom nodded, and pointed to the deli café which Jake had recommended. "Are you up for walking or would you prefer to drive?"

"I can walk. The fresh air will do me good." She messaged Jake, then they set off.

It only took a few minutes then they were inside the cozy café with its refrigerated deli offerings and china plates against the brick walls. She gestured to it. "This doesn't quite fit with the vibe I was expecting from Jake."

"He's a man of many facets."

"Who is?" a deeper voice asked.

She peeked up, her taut heartstrings easing. "You're here faster than I thought."

"I finished faster than I thought, so I was waiting nearby for your call." He sat in the seat Mom gestured to, his gaze on Poppy. "How did it go?"

She bit her lip.

He winced. "That good, huh?"

"I got the impression that Martha has some ulterior motives," Mom said. "She seems to be very interested in you, Jake."

He flushed. "She has a granddaughter she wants me to go out with." He glanced at Poppy quickly. "I haven't, just so you know."

Her heart thudded. Why he thought she needed to know that was… interesting.

"So, Martha wasn't playing, huh? I'm sorry."

"It's a beautiful space, and I could totally see myself there, but it's too expensive," Poppy admitted.

"How much does she want?"

She told him.

He flinched. "Wow."

"Exactly." Their waiter came and took their orders, and she did her best to contain the swirl of disappointment. Far from being the simple answer to prayer she'd hoped and dreamed of, this felt like an impossible hurdle. And if this was a no, then that probably meant other things were a no, too. She blinked back another rush of emotion and glanced at her place setting.

Other things. Like Jake.

JAKE CAUGHT the glistening in Poppy's eye before she ducked her head. His heart wrenched. Aw, she was upset. He'd known the studio was a good opportunity for her, but maybe he'd fueled unnecessary expectations. He wished he could hold her hand, take her someplace quiet and actually talk to her, find out what she was really thinking. But in the same breath he was grateful that Leonie was here, that she was a level head in what must be a crushing disappointment.

"I'm sorry," he murmured.

Poppy shook her head. "It's okay. I shouldn't have let myself get so excited."

"Maybe I can talk with her—"

"Oh, I don't need you to do that," she murmured as their drinks appeared.

She might think that, but it sounded like he might need to. "Hey, we'll keep knocking on the doors and one day the right door will open, yes?"

"That's right," Leonie murmured.

Poppy's smile was twisted. "I like how you say 'we.'"

"Well, it is a 'we' isn't it? You know you've got a bunch of people who care about you. And if this isn't the right one, then God has the right place for you still. Keep trusting Him."

"Amen." Leonie smiled at him.

Poppy sighed. "But this one has sprung floors."

"That's good, right?"

She rolled her eyes at him, back to the feisty Poppy he knew and loved.

That he knew and *loved*.

His hands shook, and he lowered his coffee mug with a clatter. Far from feeling mere attraction, he knew now that he'd do anything to help her. Dig into his own savings if it would bless her. He cared about her more than he cared about himself. He wanted the best for her.

Poppy eyed him. "Are you okay?"

No. It felt like a page had been turned and he was reading different words now, words that now contained an importance and significance that made everything better. *Lord, what do I do with this? What do I say to her right now? How can I encourage her?*

A face came to mind. Of course. "I think you should contact Bailey."

"Bailey? Well, yeah, I was going to show her the video I took at the place. I think she'll be jealous. Of course, there's nothing to be jealous of when I can't afford it."

"Just contact her."

"Okay." She peered at him. "Is this another of your strange sensations?"

He half shrugged. "I was just praying for you about what to do, and her face appeared in my mind. Do with that what you want."

"You're praying for me?"

"Of course, I am. All the time."

Leonie smiled at him, wearing an "aww" expression he'd seen his own mother wear at times. Usually when Ryan's baby did something. Still, better that she approved than the alternative.

Their meals arrived, and he turned the conversation to the town, its amenities, his church, the people he'd come to know.

As if overhearing him, Ben, one of his new church friends, entered and waved.

"Hey Jake. Good to see you." Ben glanced curiously at Poppy and Leonie, so Jake introduced them. "Family friends."

"Good to meet you."

"Thanks for stopping by." Jake glanced back at Poppy and Leonie. "Ben's from church."

"He seems like a nice guy."

He nodded.

"Hey, before we go, can we see your place?" Poppy asked.

"Sure." He'd tidied this morning, just on the possibility they might want to call in.

Fifteen minutes later he was standing in his driveway, helping Poppy exit. "How is your leg feeling?"

"It's letting me know it's there," she said.

"We'll do the condensed tour, then. No stairs. Well, apart from the front steps."

"Thanks." She eyed the front façade. "It's pretty."

"That's the look I was shooting for," he said dryly.

She chuckled, and his heart lifted. Maybe today could be redeemed if he could make her smile.

Leonie glanced at him. "I love how you can see the mountains everywhere in this town."

"Right? I think it's inspiring. And the tree color on the mountains is amazing."

He took them inside, and showed the front living area, the kitchen and dining space, and the back porch and yard.

Poppy smiled. "It's the perfect size for gatherings. You could get a fire pit and some Muskoka chairs and it'd be perfect."

"Good idea." And if she chose to come visit and they sat around a fire pit all night then that would be even better.

Back inside he pointed to the stairs which led to where the bedrooms, bathrooms, and other amenities were.

"You've done well," Leonie said. "It's a lot bigger than it looks like from the outside."

"Split levels do that. There's always more than meets the eye."

"Just like you," Poppy murmured.

He glanced quickly at her.

She'd reddened and turned away. "Uh, we better go soon, Mom."

"Yes, it's getting late. Jake, thank you for the chance to come visit. And for lunch, too. That was very generous."

"It's the least I can do, especially when you came all this way."

"Oh, it's not far on a good road." She ruffled Poppy's hair. "I might even be persuaded to come again someday."

"I'd like that. I'd be very happy to take you to some of the other cafes here. Or the farmers market on Saturdays."

Leonie smiled. "That's very kind of you. But I think someone else might like to come."

Poppy's smile was small. "I really appreciate you thinking of me. And lunch. And this, and everything."

"Hey, that's what friends do, right? They look out for each other."

Her blue-green eyes studied him, twin pools that reflected something he couldn't quite recognize, like a rock thrown into a pond that disturbed the depths. Was that disappointment? Possibly. But was that to do with the outcome of her meeting with Martha, or was it more to do with what he'd just said about being friends?

Now he really wished Leonie wasn't here, and he could find out what was wrong.

Poppy bit her lip. Her shoulders slumped. "That's right."

"Well, I'm going to go out to the car," Leonie said brightly, as if she'd heard his silent request before. "Thank you again for a lovely day, Jake. It's always a pleasure to see you."

"Thanks Leonie." He hugged her. "Give my best to Derek. I'm still praying for him, you know."

"Oh, you're a good boy." She patted his cheek. "I know you're older than my own son, but I still call him that sometimes too."

"I don't mind. I'd rather you think of me like that than the alternative."

She studied him, then murmured, "There is no condemnation for those who are in Christ Jesus. So as far as I'm concerned, if Jesus has made you righteous, then who am I to judge?"

He swallowed. She knew. Or had guessed the truth at least. "I'm sorry."

"I know. And she's sorry too. And you need to let her know that you don't think of her just as a friend."

His cheeks heated, as Poppy limped near from where she'd been studying his meager bookshelves. "What are you two talking about?"

"I'll see you out in the car soon." Leonie winked at him.

He mouthed a "thanks" at her then turned to Poppy. "Um, about before…"

"Which part?"

"The part about being, uh, friends."

Her lips pressed together then she ducked her head, jerked her chin. "It's okay. I know you thought this was a potential job opportunity, and I really appreciate that. I know we're only friends and didn't think anything more."

"Poppy."

She shook her head, inched away with her crutches. Then stumbled.

He rushed to catch her, cradling her close, his pulse racing. "Hey, I don't want you to fall."

She stayed there a long moment, and he grew conscious of

her breathing, of her perfect form within his arms. Memories rose. He crushed them. He loved this woman. He needed to tell her, show her, but not like before. "Poppy," he began. "I—"

She wriggled and he instantly loosed his clasp. "It's too late," she muttered.

"Too late?"

She shook her head, and pivoted away, hop-stepping her way to the door. He hurried to open it, then followed her outside, where she opened the car door and nearly fell again.

"Poppy?" Leonie asked.

Poppy ignored her, sitting then swiveling her leg inside. "Can we go please?"

What was wrong? Why was she leaving? She was leaving with his heart, too. "Poppy, please."

"Thanks for today," she said flatly, not quite looking at him, then shoving on sunglasses.

"Uh, you're welcome. I'll call you."

"Sure."

A pang crossed his heart. That didn't sound like she wanted him to. "Poppy, did I say something wrong?"

"No. I'm just tired. And disappointed. And that things I wanted didn't work out. That's all."

One of his heartstrings eased—maybe she was only disappointed about the dance studio, after all. But the way she didn't look at him suggested it was otherwise. "I'll be praying."

"Thanks." She peeked up at him finally. "Goodbye."

CHAPTER 18

The road out of Canmore took them past a rocky siding, complete with wild goats. While normally that might pique her interest, right now, she felt like her soul had flat-lined.

"Well, Canmore certainly is pretty," Mom said, clearly inviting conversation.

"Yep."

"Jake was kind, going out of his way like that."

"Yeah."

"And I really love Jake's house."

She nodded. She'd liked it too. And while it was nice to know her mother approved of him, there was no point approving a man who didn't consider himself as anything more than Poppy's friend. *Friend.* She had enough of those. What she wanted was for him to consider himself as her boyfriend. But his insistence on calling himself a friend meant she couldn't.

"So what are you thinking?"

"I don't know. I'd love to buy the studio, but it's way out of my price range."

And now, with his friend comment, even if it was affordable, saying yes to the studio would mean saying potentially yes to all the other things Canmore offered. Jake's hug might have soothed her, might have felt like coming home, but calling her a *friend* was hardly the kind of thing a girl could pin her hopes and future on. But saying all this to her mom felt like she'd expose her heart too much. So she settled for a simpler truth. "It sounds like she wants a lot."

"Maybe you should do what Jake suggested and talk to Bailey."

"Yeah."

So she did, calling her on the way home, so she wouldn't have to hear her mom sing any more of Jake's praises.

She told her about the visit, and sent the video too. "Let me know when you get it."

"It's arrived."

"Good." They must've gone through a good signal area. This part was known to be patchy at the best of times.

"Okay, I'm watching it. Oh, wow. Is that a sprung floor?"

"Yep." She shared some of what Martha had told her. "It's been here for forty years. A town institution."

"So it was made to last."

"Exactly. And it's got a little office area, and kitchenette, and bathroom facilities, even a bedroom."

"It's perfect."

"Except it costs too much."

"How much?"

She told her. Bailey clicked her tongue. "That seems an awful lot."

"That's what we thought too," Mom chipped in. "Hi Bailey."

"Hi Mrs. James. How is Mr. James?"

"On the mend."

"And how is your leg, Poppy? It must be better if they're letting you out to gallivant."

"It's hardly gallivanting when I have to use crutches still."

"But at least you're able to get out."

"True."

"Hmm, that's Luc, I need to go. But I'll keep praying for you. I know that God has an answer. And hey, every day is taking you closer to you finding that answer."

"That's a great way to look at things," Mom said.

"Thanks Bails. Take care."

"You too."

The call ended, and she soon sank into the despondency of earlier. Why would she have gotten so excited about Canmore if it wasn't meant to be? Sometimes figuring out how God worked seemed impossible. "I just don't understand."

"Don't understand what?" Mom asked.

"Well, why would Jake tell me about this place if it wasn't going to happen?"

"Who says it's not going to happen?" her mom asked. "Just because it's not right now, doesn't mean it's a forever no. It just means it's not now."

Hmm. That was a better way to look at it. "I'm trying to have faith, but it's really hard."

"It's in this waiting time, when you are wrestling with God, that faith is really found. It's too easy to claim faith when life is running smoothly."

True. "I guess this year has been a big faith builder for me, hey?"

"Exactly. And now, looking back in hindsight, there has been a number of good things that have come out of the hard times, hasn't there?"

She nodded. Like renewed faith in God. Closer family ties. And a restored friendship—she grimaced—with Jake. She couldn't regret that.

"So if God, who holds you in the palm of His hand, has proved trustworthy in the past, He is trustworthy for now too, isn't He?"

She nodded. Her faith might feel tenuous, but it was there. She knew it. "Well, I'm going to speak out God's favor, so thank You God for leading me into Your paths. And for closing the wrong doors, and opening the right ones, at the right time. Help me to trust You."

"With everything and everyone. Amen," Mom added.

"Amen." She peeked across, caught Mom's smile. "What?"

"Jake is a very nice young man."

"Mom."

"Oh, stop it. He likes you. I think he's just scared to get things wrong again. Which, to be fair, I'm secretly glad about."

"It's not a secret if you tell me, Mom."

Her mother chuckled. "I'd much rather a man take things slow with my daughter than rush ahead."

"Yeah, well, we've been there and done that—"

"I don't need to know."

Ugh. Awkward. "Mom, he called me his *friend*."

"I know."

"But I don't want to be just friends with him anymore."

"I know."

"So how do I manage this?"

"How do you think you should manage this?"

She thought about it as they traveled down the highway to Three Creek Ranch. The best thing would be to show him he meant more, instead of being so stunned that when he'd warned her about not falling she'd said it was too late. Too late because she had already fallen. Fallen for him three and a half years ago. Fallen for him again. Fallen for his kindness and patience and generous spirit. Fallen for the way he lived out his faith. Fallen for someone who seemed insistent on being so careful and cautious with her that she wondered if she'd be eighty before he'd finally find the courage to kiss her again. But saying any of that should be in person, not text, or even by phone call. Yet how could she spend time with him when he was so busy and she still couldn't drive?

"I need to see him again."

"Well, like I said before, I'm very happy to come back this way sometime. Or you can always invite him back to the ranch. I'm sure he'd be happy to come."

"He's just so busy."

"Well, Christmas is coming. You could always invite him to that."

"Really?"

"Of course. We'll have Hannah's mom, and there's always room for more."

But having Jake come to Christmas felt daring, like she was really making a statement about where she wanted this to go. And also, "That feels so far away."

"It's not that far away. And you could let him know now, so he can prioritize it."

That would certainly let him know how she felt. "Fine. I'll message him soon."

"Good. And remind him he's always welcome. I do like that young man."

"So you keep saying."

Her mother laughed. "Come on. Let's get you home."

IF JAKE COULD KICK himself he would. What kind of idiot let the woman of his dreams walk—okay, limp—on out of his life without telling her how he really felt? This kind of idiot.

He should've followed Leonie's advice and told Poppy how he felt. The fact he hadn't made him feel weak. That glorious feeling when she'd looked at him at the factory, like she thought him some kind of hero just like he'd always prayed she would, had turned tail and run away. And he was tired, so tired of this seesaw of emotion with her, the to and fro was mentally and emotionally exhausting.

"Hey God, me again. I know I messed up." He sighed. "Can You help me get this sorted with her once and for all? And if she's not meant to be for me, then please undo these heart strings so I don't care for her anymore." He opened his hands, prayed that God would set him free.

THE NEXT DAY he was at church, and surprised to have Martha bail him up again after the service. "I met your young lady friend."

"So she said."

"She's not your girlfriend?"

He wished. "No."

"Hmm. Her mother mentioned your brother and hers are friends."

"That's true."

As she eyed him, he remembered how Poppy and Leonie had remarked about her nosiness. No wonder Leonie had put the emphasis on that rather than imply he and Poppy shared a closer bond. He got the feeling Martha would not approve. "Is there something I can help you with?"

"I liked her. It's a shame she can't afford it."

"It is. I think she'd be the perfect person to take it on."

"Why?"

"Because she cares about people, and she's an excellent teacher." Or so he'd overheard at the wedding. "I think she would carry on the legacy of your studio better than anyone."

"Yet she can't afford to pay what I'm asking."

"Which is why it's a shame."

She eyed him.

He stared back. "Would it be worse to have it sitting there, never selling, or to have it sold to someone who'd just rip it apart?"

Her thin lips pressed together until they disappeared.

He shrugged. "I wonder what price you'd actually want to sell it for, to see it go to a good home."

"Why do you care so much?"

"Because I think Poppy would be an asset to this community, and I know she would take care of your studio. And believe it or not, I care about you, and I sense you'd feel better knowing it was in the capable hands of somebody who loved dance, rather than lost forever because someone wants to put in another Tim Hortons."

She shuddered. "I can't stand those places."

He shrugged. He was a fan. Timbits for the win. "So anyway, I'm just wondering how long you want to hold out for. I remember that For Sale sign being there months ago. How many interested dance people have you had come look at it?"

Her chin lifted. "That is a personal question."

"As are questions about my relationship with Poppy, yet that doesn't stop you."

"Ah, I knew it! You *are* in a relationship with her."

"No, we're only friends. To be honest, I wish we were more, but things are complicated, so we're tapping out at friends at the moment."

Her eyes squinted. "And you have no interest in my granddaughter?"

Tempting as it was to potentially try to help Poppy by saying otherwise, he knew that would be a lie. "I'm sorry, but there's only ever been one woman for me. And I messed up. She took a long time to forgive me, and now we're being friends, but I still want more."

"Poppy?"

He nodded. "Poppy. Always has been, always will be."

"So you've been faithful to her all these years?"

"I have. We broke up three years ago, and I haven't dated anyone else. I haven't kissed anyone except her."

"What, not ever?"

"Nope." He shrugged. "I guess I'm what you call a late bloomer, then I met her and felt like she was my one."

She sniffed. "I don't believe in that theory that there is only one person in the world that is right for you."

He shrugged. "Maybe there is somebody else out there, but I don't want them. I only want her."

She stared at him, and he was conscious the rest of the congregation had filtered out. He didn't blame them. This conversation with Martha felt too hard, too.

"That's actually rather sweet. My Herbert was the same. He wanted me for quite a long time, but I was too busy playing the field as we called it back in my day."

He bit his lip to suppress a smile. It was hard to imagine this wizened old woman as ever being a flirt.

"But he was always faithful to me," Martha continued, dreamily. "I never had to worry about whether he was unfaithful. I always knew when he was staying at work late that I could trust him."

"He sounds like a good man."

"He was the best." She eyed him. "So, can she trust you?"

"Absolutely."

"Hmm." She eyed him again. "If I was to come down a little in price, how much do you think she could afford?"

"Seriously?"

"I'm making no promises, mind. But I have to admit your story has touched me. As has the thought that the studio that Herbert made really should go to somebody who would appreciate it. And none of those people who inspected it so far have given me the impression that they would treasure it. Unlike your Poppy."

"She would treasure it, I know."

"So, how much do you think she can afford?"

"That I don't know. Sorry."

"Can you find out?"

He studied her, an idea springing to mind. "How much do you think you'd be willing to sell it for?"

She told him.

He did some math. "Can I check some things and get back to you soon?"

"It better be soon," she warned. "You never know who might walk through that door and want to buy it. And if they are the right kind of person, then I might be able to sell it to them."

"But they wouldn't value it like Poppy would."

"Oh, you are a conniver, aren't you?"

He shook his head. "Like I said before, I care about her, and I care about you too Martha. I want what's best for you both."

"I suspect your best for me would mean me selling it for a measly dollar."

He smiled. "Now that's a little cheap. Try two."

She cackled. "Try one million."

"Try fifty."

"Fifty? Fifty thousand? You're dreaming. Try eight hundred and fifty."

"Two hundred."

"Six."

"Four."

"Four hundred thousand?"

He nodded. "I know that's far less than what it's worth, but it would go to someone who would care for it well. Who knows? She might even be willing to keep the name if you sold it at that price."

Her eyes lit. "You really think she'd keep the name?"

"I don't know. But there's one way to find out."

"I'll need to think about this. It is freehold, after all. And close to the center of town."

"And there's a chance it might never sell to the right type of person. I guess it depends on how fast you want it to sell."

"I had thought it would've sold by now," she admitted.

"You probably could have. To someone who'd want to rip it down."

"That's cruel to remind me."

"Come on. You know it's the truth."

"Hmm." She peeked up at him. "Do you think she'd buy it before Christmas?"

"I honestly couldn't say. It depends on whether she's got access to that much money."

"Well, maybe if you would say she could make a decent offer, I might be persuaded to consider it."

"I think I can manage to talk to her."

"I would hope so. Especially if you care for her as much as you seem to think you do."

He smiled. Held out his hand. "Thank you Martha. It's been a pleasure doing business with you."

She cackled again. "I really would like to be done with this so I can move and be with my family at Christmas."

"Then let's both pray that can be done too."

CHAPTER 19

Cassie's wedding mood board had been replaced with one about a certain one-day dream dance studio. And if it just so happened to have some similar features to the place in Canmore, well, that was a coincidence. Pictures of wall colors, curtains, fonts, a little dance supplies store, she could see it so clearly, and even dreamed about it at night. Somehow the idea of owning her own studio had taken root and already she was bursting with ideas and classes. Even if the perfect site seemed far out of reach.

Her phone rang. Her heart picked up. "Bails! Hi, how are you?"

They chatted about Bailey's pregnancy—she was due soon—and then Bailey turned the conversation. "How are you doing?"

"My leg is doing better. The physiotherapist is pretty pleased."

"That's awesome! Praise God. You'll be dancing at Christmas."

"Maybe. If I can remember how to move without a cast or brace."

Bailey chuckled. "So, you know how you called up last week

and told me about the studio in Canmore that's for sale?" Bailey asked.

"Yes." The perfect studio, except it was too expensive.

"Okay, well, here's a crazy idea," Bailey said. "What if we bought it, using our capital and equity, and we considered it to be a franchise of my studio here in Winnipeg?"

Her heart flickered. "What do you mean? I didn't think things were going that well."

"Well, ever since I had to hire more teachers to replace you, things have been going gangbusters."

"Gee, thanks."

"No, don't get upset. See, it's a compliment as it took three teachers to replace one of you. Anyway, things are going really well, so there's a chance we could talk to the bank and see about getting a loan. Or I could dip into our personal savings and consider it an investment."

"I don't want a handout."

"It wouldn't be, because you remember that initial five grand you invested in my studio? Well, that'd be worth far more now. So in actual fact I probably owe you more like fifty grand by now."

Wow! "Things are going that well?"

"Poppy, I don't want you to ever think I took advantage of you when you stepped in for me during my *Dance Off* seasons. And now it looks like that time has come to an end, I'd rather pay my debts and bless you with the proceeds that I really feel you are owed."

"Have you talked to your accountant about this?"

"I have. He agrees. So there."

She laughed. "I don't know what to say."

"You could say yes. Because I think opening a studio using my name is a good option. If you were able to use a lot of our existing marketing and infrastructure then it's not like you have to feel the need to reinvent the wheel."

Good point.

"We both know how hard that is," Bailey continued, "and that you, like me, would probably prefer to be doing other things."

"Like dancing."

"We'll keep praying you can dance soon," Bailey promised.

"Thanks."

Silence stretched between them for a moment. "Hey, Poppy, did you ever think about what you might do if dancing was impossible?"

She'd dared. And instantly shut it down. "I can't even afford to go there. Everyone is saying I need to concentrate on getting well. And I'm trying to be a woman of faith about it, and not give into the doubts and fears. I'm far too good at doing that."

"You hide it well."

"And that's part of the problem. I've gotten so good at projecting this image of having it all together that when I am actually honest and real that people don't seem to want to hear it."

"I know what you mean. There's something scary about being vulnerable about things."

"Yes," she whispered.

"Well, any news about anything else?"

By 'anything else' Poppy was fairly certain Bailey was referring to men. "I'm not dating if that's what you're asking."

"Why not? Haven't you found anything more on your Dream Match app?"

She huffed. "I wish. It might work for some people but it hasn't for me."

"Nobody at church?"

"Nope."

"What about at the wedding?"

Yes. She tucked that word away.

"Poppy?"

"Oh, I didn't really do much at the wedding. My leg was sore so it wasn't like I was out there dancing every dance."

"I'm sorry."

Part of her wanted to let Bailey just feel sorry for her. But another part, the part that was trying to be more honest and real and, yes, vulnerable, knew this was another one of those opportunities to own the truth. She could pretend, or she could be real. "Actually…"

"Actually what?" Bailey nearly squealed.

"I did manage to dance a couple of dances."

"Who with? Oh, don't go disappointing me and saying it was an uncle or a cousin."

"What about a brother?" she teased.

She could nearly hear the disappointment flowing down the line. "Look, we know Franklin is a good guy, but that's not what I meant either."

"I didn't mean Franklin."

"Ooh! Well, whose brother then?"

She swallowed. Finally dared. "Ryan Guillemette's."

"Poppy!"

She winced. Was that judgment?

"I want to know *all* the details."

Oh no she didn't.

"Look, let's just say we dated super briefly when I was back in Calgary."

"And you're only telling me this now?"

"It didn't end well, and then we didn't see each other again until recently. Then he saved my dad's life, as you probably know, and Dad insisted he come to the wedding. And we danced, and talked, and yeah. Things seem a lot better now."

"Oh my gosh! It's like a second chance for you both."

"It would be, if he hadn't insisted on saying we were only friends."

"What?"

"Look, it's okay. I guess it means I'm free to go find a date of my own, which is why I thought I'd try a dating app. But yeah, I thought you'd find that interesting."

"You know I love a good romance, but this one sounds a little complicated for me."

"Try living it," Poppy muttered.

"Oh, you poor thing."

"Yeah, it's not been easy. So, that's what's been happening. Have fun praying about all of that."

"Oh, Poppy."

She shook her head. "Enough of that. How are you? How is that baby going? I hope you know I plan on being an honorary aunty."

"That's not even a question."

Bailey shared, and Poppy listened and smiled, praying for her friend when Bailey soon hung up. Poppy needed to stay outward focused, others focused, even as so much remained uncertain in her own life. At least the doctor was optimistic this operation really had worked and would see her leg healed. Which was great. But again raised the question of what to do next.

And the question of what to do about the studio remained. Yes, Bailey's offer of the fifty grand would definitely help boost her savings, but was it enough to convince a bank to give her a loan? And yes, opening a studio under Bailey's name was kindly meant, but again it felt like she was only the supporting act, propping up somebody else again, and not the main event. Was that prideful to think that way? Or was that what God wanted?

"Lord, I would really like to know what Your plans are."

No answer, but there wasn't that sense of prayers hitting the ceiling like she'd felt not so long ago. Instead, she felt like her Heavenly Father heard, that He understood. And the trust she'd been cultivating in recent days and weeks was like a bedrock she could stand on.

Whatever happened, now she *knew* that God was in control.

Her phone bleeped a message. She checked it. Only Hannah. She tapped back a response, then checked her last message to Jake. Had it been too vague? She read it again.

> Thanks for today. Appreciate you. Let me know if you're ever heading past this way again. Be great to see you again.

Maybe she hadn't been clear enough. She could try again.

> Been thinking of you. Praying all is going well. Wanted to know if you felt like visiting for Christmas, either to or from your folks. Love to see you. I miss you.

There. He'd have to know how she felt with that, wouldn't he?

So she pressed send.

HIS HEART SKIPPED A BEAT. Another two. She wanted him to come see her? Spend Christmas there? Okay, he might've been a little clueless about a lot of things, but even he could understand what she meant by that invitation.

He tapped out a reply.

> I'd love to see you too. Miss you as well. Would be good to see you sooner than Christmas though.

Her response came back almost immediately.

> What about this weekend?

He smiled.

> What about tonight?

Tonight? I haven't washed my hair!

> I don't care. I promise not to look. I need to talk to you about something.

What?

> Uh uh. It'd be better to talk in person.

Sounds serious.

> Yeah, you could say that. Don't worry. It's a good thing.

Okay then. Tonight at my house?

> I'll finish work at six so can be there at seven if that works.

I'll save you some dinner?

> Yes please.

Jake smiled. Finally they were getting somewhere.

HE PULLED in outside the Three Creek Ranch house at five minutes past seven. It was dark, cold, but as soon as he saw the woman stand from the rocking chair on the front porch all fatigue faded. He jumped out of his car, and she let the blanket fall to the floor and hobbled to him.

"Hi." She smiled and stretched out her arms.

"Hi." He folded her inside, earning a little squeak. Okay, so he shouldn't hold her quite so tight. But this moment in the darkness, save for the light spilling from an uncurtained window pooling gold on the porch, felt special, private, like it was just the two of them.

"I missed you," she murmured.

"It's only been five days."

"That's nearly a week. Far too long. I think needing to see you is becoming addictive."

He smiled. "I know what you mean."

She pulled back, peered up at him. "Do you mean that?"

"Sure do." His words came out more gravelly than he intended.

Maybe she heard that tone too, for her eyes swept to his mouth then back up again.

His heart kicked. He'd really like to spill the news that Martha had shared the other day, but another part of him held back, hoping that she would finally admit how she felt, rather than wait until he shared something that might prove celebratory rather than revelatory.

He stroked her cheek. Lowered his face. Saw her eyes widen.

"Jake." Her voice was a whisper.

"Poppy."

Her smile held an invitation. "Is that what you came to say?"

"No." His brain grew fuzzy, blurry. What had he come to say? All at once something he knew he *had* to say came to mind. "I love you."

Her breath hitched. "Jake."

"I realized it the other day. Then realized that there's only ever been one woman for me. And you're her. And I had to come to tell you that. I hope you don't mind."

"Mind?" Her eyes darkened as she smiled. "I don't mind at all."

Then she tugged his head down and lifted her face and met his lips with her own.

Oh, the sheer pleasure of touching her lips. The sheer joy of feeling like he was where he belonged. That they were made for each other. Crafted by God for each other. And though they'd stumbled, God had proved faithful, protecting one another for each other ever since.

Her hand slid up his neck into his hair, sending sensations down his spine. Then he felt other sensations stir, so pulled back, eyeing her, his breaths unsteady.

She stared back, her gaze heavy-lidded. "I'd forgotten how well you kiss."

"I hadn't."

She smirked.

"It's why I've had to be so careful around you. Because I didn't want to hurt you again."

She shook her head. "The only way you can hurt me is by insisting we're only friends."

"I know. That was dumb. I'm sorry. I did try to rectify things but I was too late."

"You were definitely too late. That horse had bolted, leaving one very bruised dancer in its wake."

"I'm sorry." He brushed another kiss across her lips.

"Are you trying to kiss me better?"

"Is it working?" He kissed her again.

"Maybe."

He chuckled, then noticed she was shivering. "Hey, we should get you inside."

"I'm fine."

He gestured to the blanket. "How long were you waiting outside?"

"Only for five minutes."

"You didn't have to do that."

"I know. But I also kind of did."

"Why's that?"

"Because I didn't want to miss a second when you got here. I've missed too many over the past years."

"But this is our second chance, right?"

She nodded. "A second chance for this dancer."

"*My* dancer," he murmured.

She smiled. "I love you."

His heart sang. "Really?"

"Really."

Her answer could only be met with another kiss, this one longer, which was only broken when the door opened, forcing them apart. "Come on you two," Jess said. "We all saw the car arrive hours ago."

"Hours?"

"Okay, ten minutes ago. But it's cold, so get inside and warm up. Even though it looks pretty hot out here." She smirked.

Poppy touched her swollen lips and he pressed a kiss to her brow. "Sorry if I messed up your lipstick."

"I'm not."

He laughed. Yes, this was more of the feisty Poppy he recalled.

He entered, holding her hand, and said hello to Leonie (who hugged him) and Derek (who shook his hand) and Jess, who smirked and gestured to her lip.

He followed her movement and found a smear of Poppy's lipstick on his mouth. Oops. That must've been fun for Derek to see.

Poppy tugged him to the kitchen table, where plates for two waited.

"The others aren't joining us?"

She shook her head. "They wanted to, but I insisted on having you all to myself."

"I can't say I'm sorry about that outcome."

"Good." She wrinkled her nose. "If I was all better I'd go over and prove my domestic goddess skills by serving you some food. As I'm not, you'll just have to say nice things about the meal."

"Did you cook?"

"Lamb shanks. My specialty. The one thing I know how to cook. I hope you like it."

"If you made it, I'll love it." And he'd eat every morsel, no matter how it tasted.

But when he did finally taste it, he had to ask for seconds. "This is really good."

"Right? I saw it in a recipe book and it's so easy but so good, especially in a slow cooker. Especially when it's cold outside."

He trapped her hand in his, threaded her fingers through his own. "I like feeling like we're together again."

"Me too," she whispered.

Her look was begging for another kiss, but he refrained, conscious her parents were in the room next door and might walk through any second. Which was also kindly helpful in cooling his ardor, and proved why chaperones were not such a dumb idea after all.

Poppy picked up his hand and kissed his knuckles. "Can I say I'm very glad you decided to call by and say all this?"

He grinned, then a sharp realization of what he'd actually meant to say, before getting waylaid with other important things, came back to mind. "Actually, that's not all I needed to say."

"There's more?" Her eyes widened.

"Not like that," he mumbled, his cheeks heating. "It's about the dance studio."

Her expression grew cautious. "What about it?"

"I think Martha might've had a change of heart."

"How so?"

He told her about Martha's comments the other day, then about the message she'd sent today. "So the fact she's now willing to consider that offer to ensure it goes to a good home, well, I thought you might like to hear that in person."

"Are you serious?"

He nodded.

"I can't believe it." Her eyes were huge.

"It feels like a miracle, doesn't it?"

She nodded. "You know how you asked me to call Bailey? I did and she offered to take it on as a secondary studio."

"Wow. And do you want to?"

Her nose wrinkled. "I feel like it makes me a bad friend to say no, but I don't really want to."

"She's offered to buy it?"

"Yes. But she's also offered me fifty thousand, as a thank you for what I did when I looked after the studio for her when she had to go on the TV show."

"Maybe that's why you had to call her."

"Is it bad of me to want to take the money and not her name? I just want to have something that's mine. Does that make me selfish?"

"No."

She sighed. "I have to admit that since it was first suggested the thought of having my own studio has tantalized more and more. Setting my own hours, making my own decisions about the space and what classes we could offer. I want to do that, and earn my own success instead of trading on someone else's reputation."

"I understand completely."

Her lips slanted. "I suppose you do. It's the curse of having more famous siblings, isn't it? We always feel like we have to prove ourselves."

"Until we realize we really don't, and that God has got things under control."

She drew in a deep breath, released it, and nodded. "You're so good to remind me."

"That's because I love you."

"Aww."

His attention flew to where Jess stood, hand on her heart, leaning against the doorway. "Young love."

Old love, rekindled.

"Is there something we can help you with?" Poppy asked.

"Only by telling me how long this has been going on for."

"Since he drove up."

"Just tonight?" Jess squealed, and Benji, the Golden Labrador, who he'd seen several times before, bounded up. "Then it really *is* young love."

"You know we used to date before."

"Yes, but I'm gonna guess that wasn't love."

Maybe.

Jess smirked. "So, what else is going on?"

"You could tell her about the studio."

"What about the studio?"

Poppy smiled. "Jake came to tell me that Martha has had a change of heart and is willing to drop the price to make sure the studio goes to a good home."

"Yay!" Jess clapped her hands. "That's awesome. But can you afford it?"

Poppy nodded. "I think so, now with the extra money that Bailey is sending me."

"What extra money?"

Poppy told her, which drew another excited squeal, which in turn caused Benji to bark and brought Leonie and Derek out to see what the fuss was about.

"Poppy is going to buy her studio after all."

"You are?" Leonie asked.

Poppy explained again about Martha's reduced offer.

Leonie's mouth dropped. "What caused her to change her mind?"

"God?" he suggested.

"God, and possibly you, am I right?" Poppy sent him a look.

He shrugged. "I simply reminded her that selling it to someone who would appreciate and value it would potentially be a better option than never selling."

"Thank you, thank you, thank you." She rocketed from her chair and kissed him.

After a too-short encounter with her lips, he met Derek's bemused look, and Leonie and Jess's "aww" faces.

Then he remembered, and glanced back at Poppy. "Uh, she did say she'd prefer it if you could keep the Diamond name. I think she wants to keep her legacy alive." He winced. "And I know you want to be known for yourself, and not trade on anyone else's success."

Her nose wrinkled. "Do you think it's a hard no if I don't? Because let's be honest, the space is great, but her business has been closed for two years. It's not exactly a success."

"Maybe there's a way you can show her the Diamond legacy is still being honored in some way so she might be okay with that."

"Like a plaque inside," Jess suggested.

"Or a scholarship in her name," Leonie said.

"Ooh, I like those ideas." Poppy looked at him. "I should go see her again, shouldn't I?"

"I think she's the kind of woman who might change her mind if given too long to think about it."

Poppy nodded. "So I should go to the bank first thing and make sure I have enough to take out a loan."

He cleared his throat. "I have some savings you can use as well if you want."

"What? I couldn't take your money."

"You wouldn't be taking it. It's an investment."

"I know what kind of investment Jake's hoping for," Jess murmured.

He glanced at her. Stuck out his tongue. Shook his head as the others laughed, and Poppy stared at him with pink cheeks.

But he didn't care. He'd found his Poppy years ago, and now would do anything to bless her. Contributing financially to her studio was a small price to pay. And regardless of whether she agreed to the long term investment that Jess alluded to, he'd continue to bless her all the rest of his days. Because that was what love did.

EPILOGUE

Christmas

There was something so special about sitting here with all the people she loved best in the world. Apart from Bailey and little Emily, everyone else was here. She clutched Jake's hand. He'd joined her, along with his family and Sylvie and Ryan's new son.

There were a lot of babies in her world. Hannah and Franklin's newborn daughter had come a little earlier than expected, but was doing well.

"You know, I thought Thanksgiving was a time to celebrate all the wonderful things that God has been doing, but it just feels like there's so much more now." Poppy raised her leg, pointed her toe. "Like praise God for legs that finally work."

"Amen."

"And praise God for new dance studios."

"Yay!" Cassie applauded.

"Canmore won't know what hit it," Harrison declared.

"I can't wait to open in the new year."

After a frantic few weeks renovating, painting, installing

new signage, the Poppy James Dance Studio would be opening its doors in two weeks' time. She couldn't wait.

"Praise God for former dance studio owners being excited about scholarships offered in their name so they lower the price," Jake said.

"Amen!"

"And praise God for patient boyfriends who helped negotiate a lower price in the first place." Poppy kissed his cheek.

"Jake the Great!" Cassie smiled.

"And praise God for patient boyfriends who are ready for a wedding next year!" Jess called.

"You picked a date?" Harrison asked.

"I told you this," Cassie teased.

"Sorry, it's been a big few months."

"Ooh, that's right. Praise God for Harrison getting the leading man role in the new Ainsley Beckett movie."

"Yay!"

"And praise God for Ainsley Beckett insisting I get that role," Harrison said, grinning.

"God bless her."

"And praise God for this little one's arrival." Franklin kissed his newborn's head who looked around with sleepy eyes.

This produced a more muted chorus of yays and Amens.

Then Jake turned to Poppy. "And praise God for giving us second chances."

"Amen," she murmured.

"And praise God for patient boyfriends, but actually... I'm not one of them."

She blinked. "You're not?"

He shook his head. The table quietened. "I think everyone here knows that we once dated. And that things didn't end well. And we spent too long apart. And I don't want to waste another moment without you. So Poppy James," he held her hand, "I know that it's been a long and winding journey, but I'd really like to spend the rest of my life with you. To do life together, through the ups and the downs. I know Martha hasn't always been easy to deal with, but I hope that we can share a love like she and Herbert did. Like your parents do. That lasts through thick and thin—"

"Is he calling your dad fat?" Tom whispered loudly to Jess.

"Shh!" Poppy kept her eyes on Jake. "Go on."

"And while you might have bought the Diamond studio, I hope you'll accept this diamond too." He drew out a ring.

She gasped. Was he serious? The size of that diamond certainly suggested he was.

"I love you Poppy. Will you marry me?"

"Of course I will." She threw herself into his arms. "Yes, yes, yes. All the yesses in the world."

He laughed, and she kissed him, as around them people cheered, catcalled, and little Jonah cried.

But that was the sound of love. The sound of family. The sound of joy.

And as Jake pushed the diamond ring onto her finger, and kissed her without caring about the table's comments, she knew that while this dancer might now have a diamond, it was the knowledge that she was loved that meant most of all.

She was loved by Jake. Loved by her family. Loved by her friends. And loved by God. And who could want anything more?

If you enjoyed this book, please leave a review at your place of purchase. Want more books like this? Then check out Carolyn's website at www.carolynmillerauthor.com

A NOTE FROM THE AUTHOR

Thank you for reading *A Second Chance for a Dancer*, the third book in the Three Creek Ranch romance series, that follows *A Cameo for a Cowgirl*, and *A Valentine for a Vet*. This is another of those 'accidental' series, where characters from *Fire and Ice* (Franklin and Hannah's story) took on a life of their own and demanded to have their stories told. So in this series we see Franklin's three sisters negotiate love and life and how that links to their family ranch.

Three Creek Ranch with its Western Town and Back Lot is actually based on a real ranch and movie set just outside Calgary, which has been the setting of all kinds of movies and TV shows, from *Lonesome Dove* to *Shanghai Noon* to *When Calls the Heart* and *Heartland*. I had *way* too much fun imagining what it must be like to manage a similar ranch and movie set, and have spent many an hour checking out the CL Western Town and Backlot site.

Readers who have been keeping up to date with my books may enjoy a few references to other characters, such as Ryan and Sylvie, who we got to know in *The Love Penalty* and Bailey from *Pointe, Shoots, and Scores*.

A NOTE FROM THE AUTHOR

To find out more about these books and behind-the-scenes inspiration, and to sign up for my newsletter, please visit my website at www.carolynmillerauthor.com

Big thanks to May from Christian Shelves for her Canadian insights, and to Brittany, Evelyn, Christie and the other ladies in my ARC and review team.

Reviews help other readers find new-to-them authors, so if you can spare a moment to write a quick review at Amazon / Goodreads / your place of purchase, I'd be very grateful.

If you enjoy Christian contemporary romance you may want to check out the books in the Original Six hockey romance series, a sweet & swoony, slightly sporty Christian contemporary romance series.

The Breakup Project
Love on Ice
Checked Impressions
Hearts and Goals
Big Apple Atonement
Muskoka Blue

Romance fans who enjoy small town life may also enjoy reading the Muskoka Romance series, that starts with *Muskoka Shores*.

And if you need more small town stories, check out those in the Greener Gardens collections.

I'd love for you to check out my other books and to sign up for my newsletter at www.carolynmillerauthor.com where you

A NOTE FROM THE AUTHOR

can be the first to learn all my book and contest news, and discover more behind-the-book details and photos. Newsletter subscribers can also get an exclusive bonus book free, so grab your copy of *Originally Yours* here.

May God bless you - and happy reading!
    Carolyn

ABOUT THE AUTHOR

Carolyn Miller lives in the beautiful Southern Highlands of New South Wales, Australia, with her husband and four children. A longtime lover of romance, especially that of Jane Austen, Georgette Heyer and LM Montgomery, Carolyn loves to write contemporary and historical romance that draws readers into fictional worlds that show the truth of God's grace in our lives.

To find out more about Carolyn's books, and to subscribe to her newsletter, please visit www.carolynmillerauthor.com. By subscribing, you can also get a free novella, Originally Yours.

You can also connect with her at

ALSO BY CAROLYN MILLER

Contemporary:

<u>The Original Six hockey series</u>
The Breakup Project
Love on Ice
Checked Impressions
Hearts and Goals
Big Apple Atonement
Muskoka Blue

<u>Northwest Ice hockey series</u>
Fire and Ice
The Love Penalty
Pointe, Shoots, and Scores
Faking the Shot
Plays By the Book
Second Shot at Love
On a Wing and a Prayer

<u>Three Creeks Ranch Romance series</u>
A Cameo for a Cowgirl
A Valentine for a Vet
A Second Chance for the Dancer

<u>Muskoka Romance series</u>
Muskoka Shores

Muskoka Christmas

Muskoka Hearts

Muskoka Spotlight

Muskoka Holiday Morsels

Muskoka Promise

Muskoka Miracle

Trinity Lakes collection

Love Somebody Like You

Tangled Up in Love

Only You Can Love Me

Our House on Sycamore Street

The Lost Daughter's Irishman

The Fairall Romance Legacy

An Irish Kiss

An Irish Hope

An Irish Wish

The Greener Gardens Romance series

Restoring Fairhaven

Regaining Mercy

Reclaiming Hope

Rebuilding Hearts

Refining Josie

The Silver Teapot Series

Not Exactly Mr Darcy

Not Precisely Mr Knightley

Not So Very Sensible

Historical:

<u>Regency Wallflowers</u>
Dusk's Darkest Shores
Midnight's Budding Morrow
Dawn's Untrodden Green

<u>Regency Brides: Legacy of Grace</u>
The Elusive Miss Ellison
The Captivating Lady Charlotte
The Dishonorable Miss DeLancey

<u>Regency Brides: Promise of Hope</u>
Winning Miss Winthrop
Miss Serena's Secret
The Making of Mrs Hale

<u>Regency Brides: Daughters of Aynsley</u>
A Hero for Miss Hatherleigh
Underestimating Miss Cecilia
Misleading Miss Verity

'Heaven and Nature Sing' from the Joy to the World Christmas novella collection

'More than Gold' from
the Across the Shores novella collection

'Convincing the Circuit Preacher' from
The Courting the Country Preacher novella collection

www.ingramcontent.com/pod-product-compliance
Lightning Source LLC
LaVergne TN
LVHW040048080526
838202LV00045B/3542